JANET TRONSTAD

grew up on a small farm in central Montana. One of her favorite things to do was to visit her grandfather's bookshelves, where he had a large collection of Zane Grey novels. She's always loved a good story. Today Janet lives in Pasadena, California where she is a full-time writer.

DEBRA CLOPTON

was a 2004 Golden Heart finalist in the inspirational category, a 2006 Inspirational Readers Choice Award winner, a 2007 Golden Quill award winner and a finalist for the 2007 American Christian Fiction Writers Book of the Year Award. She praises the Lord each time someone votes for one of her books, and takes it as an affirmation that she is exactly where God wants her to be.

Debra is a hopeless romantic and loves to create stories with lively heroines and the strong heroes who fall in love with them. But most importantly she loves showing her characters living their faith, seeking God's will in their lives one day at a time. Her goal is to give her readers an entertaining story that will make them smile, hopefully laugh and always feel God's goodness as they read her books. She has found the perfect home for her stories writing for the Love Inspired line and still has to pinch herself just to see if she really is awake and living her dream.

When she isn't writing she enjoys taking road trips, reading and spending time with her two sons, Chase and Kris. She loves hearing from readers and can be reached through her Web site, www.debraclopton.com, or P.O. Box 1125, Madisonville, Texas 77864.

Small-Town Brides
Janet Tronstad &
Debra Clopton

Steeple
Hill®

Published by Steeple Hill Books™

STEEPLE HILL BOOKS

Steeple
Hill®

Recycling programs
for this product may
not exist in your area.

ISBN-13: 978-0-373-87531-3

SMALL-TOWN BRIDES

Copyright © 2009 by Harlequin Books S.A.

The publisher acknowledges the copyright holders of the individual works
as follows:

A DRY CREEK WEDDING
Copyright © 2009 by Janet Tronstad

A MULE HOLLOW MATCH
Copyright © 2009 by Debra Clopton

www.SteepleHill.com

Printed in U.S.A.

CONTENTS

A DRY CREEK WEDDING
Janet Tronstad

With love to my old friend, Jim Jett.

And we know that all things work together for good to them that love God, to them who are the called according to His purpose.

—*Romans* 8:28

Chapter One

Clay Preston hated to get involved in other people's problems. But he held out the foil-wrapped hamburger to the woman sitting next to him anyway. "Here. You have to eat something."

He and Rene Mitchell were in his tow truck in the parking lot of a fast-food place north of Denver. The sky was overcast and the clerk inside had mentioned the possibility of a late snowstorm coming down from Canada. Unless they hurried, Clay figured they'd be driving right into that blizzard. He should be worried about icy roads instead of, well, *her*.

Rene looked up at him indignantly. She'd been drumming her fingers on her jean-clad leg until she stopped to stare at him like he'd said something insensitive.

Clay gritted his teeth. "I know. Love's done you wrong. And you don't feel like eating anything. But you have to."

Clay was glad none of his old buddies could see him now. They had given him a hard time when he left the rodeo to start a towing business. They said he'd get tired of rescuing fools on the road and be back to riding for the prize in no time.

They'd have a good laugh if they knew he was playing nursemaid to one of his customers. He had hoisted her car onto the back of his truck two days ago, and that's when his troubles had started.

"You've never been in love, so you don't know how it feels," Rene said with a catch in her voice. Shadows gathered in the cab, but he could still see her misery more clearly than he wanted.

"I know enough to know a body needs to eat." Sheer desperation had made him tell her more about himself than he intended. The radio in the truck didn't work and, if they weren't talking, Rene was sitting there muttering to herself about that boyfriend of hers and the state of love in general.

Clay reminded himself it was the fear of her fainting—in *his* truck—that made him press her to eat the burger. He didn't even want to know the amount of paperwork he'd need to fill out if he had to take her to some local hospital.

"The heart might not need food, but the stomach does," Clay finally said. Sentimental clichés were not his style, but he didn't know what else to say. The woman didn't listen to reason. He suddenly wondered if that might be because she had low blood sugar or something.

He glanced out the window to see if there were any medical buildings nearby. There weren't. Darkness was settling in and all he saw out of the ordinary were a couple of flakes of snow that were melting as they hit his windshield. It wasn't enough to make him worry quite yet. He turned back to look at his passenger.

"I'm not in love anymore," Rene said, her lips pressing tight together before she added, "I've given the whole thing up."

Clay nodded. He figured that attitude would last until

her boyfriend, Trace Crawford, got back from wherever he had gone and found out that Rene had left town. Trace must be on a trip buying cattle or something. That was the only reason Clay could think of to explain the man's continued absence. Most men would be heating up the highways to keep a woman like Rene.

Of course, Clay knew not to press her on it. He felt helpless about her crying and, here she was, blinking back tears again.

"I'm sure Trace will call," he offered stiffly. He was no good at playing Dear Abby. He shouldn't even try.

Rene didn't say anything. She didn't reach out and take the burger, either.

Clay had first noticed Rene when she was a waitress at the café in the small town of Mule Hollow. He'd just moved to Texas so he hadn't known anyone there except his uncle, who owned the local garage. It was Uncle Prudy who had sold him this tow truck and told him to use the garage credit card to buy gas for this trip. His uncle believed in taking care of the people of his town, and he had insisted Clay take Rene where she needed to go. His uncle had even assured him he would use his old tow truck to handle any calls in Clay's absence.

The older man had said Clay should look at this as a little vacation. A time to relax. To get to know a nice girl.

Uncle Prudy had enough sense not to say the rest of what he was thinking, but then he didn't need to. His hopes had come through loud and clear over the phone without him uttering a word.

Clay had just shaken his head. The older man might as well go outside and spit in the wind. That's how much chance Clay had with a woman like Rene and, frankly, it was more chance than he wanted. Happy or sad, she gushed with emotions, and he didn't have a clue what to do with any of them.

"I wouldn't worry about Trace," he finally said to her. That seemed safe enough.

"I'm not." Rene turned to look out the window.

Clay wished his uncle could see him and Rene right now. The sight of her huddled against the passenger door, looking more dejected by the minute, would stop any illusions his uncle had. If Clay couldn't convince Rene to eat when she was hungry, he had no hope of persuading her to settle down with him in marital bliss. Not that he believed there was such a thing even if she did.

Oh, he wasn't opposed to marriage. That's what kept the world civilized. Falling in love, on the other hand, always seemed an awkward thing to him. It was like a temporary madness that took hold of people and wrung them dry, usually after making utter fools out of them.

Clay wasn't naïve. He knew lust could drive a man to do some crazy things. He could understand that. He could even grasp why men made commitments to kids and a family. That was kind of noble. What he could never understand, though, was the kind of romantic nonsense that was plaguing the woman sitting next to him.

He wished he had realized where things stood between Rene and Trace a little sooner. Maybe then he'd know what to do now. Of course, he had seen them flirt with each other in the café, but he hadn't noticed that it had gotten serious. And he should have seen it coming. He had been watching Rene since the day he first saw her moving around the tables in the café.

He smiled slightly just remembering it. With her soft

blond hair and willowy shape, she was like a golden butterfly, dipping here to pour a cup of coffee and sliding
there to give someone else more toast. She sparkled with
silver filigree jewelry and her eyes danced as she moved.
She was a sight to behold.

His first clue that she was even dating had been when
Rene stormed out of town hours after she had that argument
with Trace. And Clay only knew about the quarrel because
he overheard a couple of the old ladies in town muttering
about Trace's botched proposal as they walked past the
open door of Uncle Prudy's garage.

Clay had smelled the heavy exhaust from Rene's car as
he watched her leave that day, so he figured she would be
calling Trace soon enough to go get her. The minute that
muffler fell off she wouldn't know what to do. Most women
liked to be rescued by their boyfriends, even if they were mad
at them, so Clay told himself his butterfly would be back at
the café in time to serve him breakfast. Trace would apolo-
gize and give her whatever she wanted and the wedding
plans would move forward. It was as inevitable as spring.

If Clay had felt a twinge of disappointment that Rene
was going to be married, he pushed it aside.

When the call came, it had been directed to his tow
truck number. Clay had just added the toll-free number to
his cell phone so it took a couple of seconds for him to
realize it was Rene who wanted him to tow her car.

Business wasn't good enough that he could afford to
ignore paying customers, not even ones who made him
nervous. All the way out to her car, he kept expecting to
get a call telling him that she'd finally decided to contact
Trace and didn't need a tow any longer. But his cell phone
was silent.

When he got to Rene's car, he had seen that the problem was bigger than the muffler.

Clay had known at the time he should have insisted that he tow her car back to his uncle's garage. But Rene had started protesting in earnest when he mentioned returning to Mule Hollow, saying she was never going back there. Clay could have stood her fuming, but she looked like she might cry, too. So he said he'd tow her to the next garage farther along the road, closer to where she was going—

"Dry Creek, Montana," Rene had said when he asked her.

Looking back, Clay knew that first compromise had been his fatal mistake. He should have asked Rene about her finances before he'd made his offer. If he'd known, he could have told her none of the garages ahead would give someone who was just passing through thirty days to pay her bill. By the time he knew how broke she was, he was already committed. He'd promised his uncle to see this crazy journey through to the end.

Clay looked up at Rene again. He couldn't have abandoned her anyway. Not when she needed help.

"It's got grilled onions on it." He figured he might as well make one last attempt to reason with her. Then he set the burger down on the seat between them so he could pick up his own and eat it in peace.

Rene tried not to look at the hamburger. Her stomach was so empty it had started rumbling. It was surprising she could think about food at all considering the dismal state of her life, but there it was. Apparently, Clay was right about one thing. Being brokenhearted didn't always kill a person's appetite.

She forced herself to smile politely at the man. "Thank you very much. But I—"

She gave a vague wave of her hands that could mean anything. Mostly, it meant she didn't want to be any more beholden to Clay and his uncle than she already was. She'd left most of her money in Mule Hollow so her cousin could pay the rent on the house they shared. Rene had planned to use her credit card on this trip, but something had happened and her last payment had never reached the credit card company so her card was not accepting new charges. The payment to her cell phone company hadn't gotten there, either. She'd used the last of her cash to pay for her motel room last night.

Clay frowned. "You have to be hungry."

"I can wait until we get to Dry Creek." She was in the food business; she knew people could live for weeks without eating. Some people voluntarily went on fasts that lasted for days. Besides, while Clay had been down the street getting gas this morning, she'd had a donut and a cup of coffee in the motel's lobby. In some countries, that was a full day's calorie intake.

"Suit yourself. I won't mind eating two burgers."

Rene wouldn't have minded eating two of those hamburgers, either. The smell of them filled the cab. And she loved grilled onions; she'd told Clay that when she refused a different burger yesterday. Of course, then she hadn't been hungry. Now, it would be so easy to reach out and take what he offered.

But if she was going to stand on her own, she might as well start now.

Life, she had to admit, wasn't going the way she had imagined it would. She'd thought she had it all figured out, especially the love part. Rene had heard about falling in love since she was a toddler. Her grandparents and her parents had all fallen in love at first sight. Everyone in the family found their mates that way.

Rene had felt that light, floating sensation when she first saw Trace. She was thirty-two years old, and it had been the first time she'd had that feeling so she thought it had to mean something. Obviously, she wasn't gifted with the same radar that the other women in her family had. Trace didn't love her at all.

She wasn't going to rely on her feelings any longer. She planned to take a dozen good looks at a man before she thought about love again. And then she was going to make her decision based on cold, hard facts. She might even make a list of requirements for a spouse. No more of this head spinning for her.

She could no longer trust all of the stories she'd heard growing up. In the past one hundred years, every bride in her family had fallen in love with their husbands the first time they looked into their faces. They all reported having that floating, spinning feeling and it had been the real thing. They were in love and their men loved them back. They all had fairy tale weddings and wore the white lace wedding veil her great-grandmother had made.

Rene had grown up expecting to have a grand romance like the rest of the women in her family. While her mother told her the stories, Rene would sit and dream about the veil. The veil was edged with blue forget-me-nots, which, the stories all claimed, symbolized true love for every bride who wore it.

After her mother died, Rene and her cousin, Paisley, had inherited the veil. When the two of them had moved to Mule Hollow a few months ago, they'd brought the veil with them. Paisley claimed to be so focused on her new teaching job that she wasn't interested in dating, but Rene had hoped the small town would be a good place for them to find God-fearing husbands. After all, the town was so overrun with cowboy bachelors a female reporter even wrote a column about it. That had to be a good sign.

"If it makes you feel better, we could add the hamburger to the tab you're running for my towing services," Clay said as he took another bite of his hamburger.

"I'll be fine," Rene said. "Don't worry about me."

They were silent for a minute and then Rene's stomach growled.

"Trace would take the burger," Clay said.

"You don't know what he'd do." Rene had noticed Clay and Trace sometimes sat in the café at the same time, but the two men hadn't seemed to know each other.

Clay grunted in a noncommittal fashion.

"You don't, do you? Know him, I mean?" She panicked before assuring herself she would have remembered if the two men had greeted each other with more than a nod. They were both striking people. Even when she was falling in love with Trace, she'd noticed Clay. He had a certain glint to his eyes that made her wonder sometimes. Of course, he wore his Stetson pulled so low over his face that his eyes were generally in the shadows, so she couldn't see them clearly. And he had grunted more than he spoke when she waited on him in the café.

Just then, Clay tipped his Stetson back and gave her a slow, lazy smile. "After listening to you for the better part of two days, I should hope I know what your intended is like."

Now that his hat was out of the way, she could see a little too clearly. Golden flecks gathered in his moss-colored eyes. He had a day's growth of dark whiskers on his strong face. That, along with an old scar along his cheek, made him look rugged. Like a warrior or a—

Rene felt a flush creep up her neck. "He isn't my intended. I never said yes."

Clay didn't say anything else, so Rene wondered if the two men did know each other better than she thought.

"Not that there's anything wrong with him," she added, just in case.

She didn't want Clay to think badly of her for criticizing some friend of his, but he had to see that the quality of Trace's affection had been lacking. After all, the other man had proposed to her in one breath and then, in the next, confessed that he needed a wife so he'd have someone to take care of the niece he was bringing to live with him. Any woman had a right to expect more than that from a man who wanted to marry her.

"He'd still take the burger," Clay said.

Rene suddenly knew that was true. She was being a fool. Trace wasn't going hungry because things hadn't worked out between them. He was probably eating a double cheeseburger at the café in Mule Hollow right now—and chatting up any woman foolish enough to be sitting next to him.

Rene picked up the burger. "Just be sure you add it to your bill."

"You can count on it," Clay said with satisfaction in his voice. "You're going to owe me your first month's pay at the rate we're going anyway. Even with the good-customer discount I'm giving you."

"I'm a good customer?" Rene looked to see if the teasing was back in Clay's eyes, but his hat was pulled down again. "Really?"

"You will be when you pay up."

Ah, yes, money, Rene thought. She was not always the best provider for herself. Which reminded her. She took a quick moment to bow her head. Thanks for the burger, God. And bless us on this trip. Amen.

She didn't want to make a big production about praying. Although Clay wore a tiny gold cross pinned to his hat band, she'd never seen him pray when he ate at the café. Of course, she wasn't a poster child for prayer herself these days. Bowing her head before eating had become more habit than anything since her mother had died.

"Yum." Rene took a bite of food. It tasted as good as it smelled. "This is wonderful. Thank you."

"You pray a lot?" Clay asked after she swallowed.

"Some days." Rene said. Clay didn't need to know about her crumbling relationship with God. It wasn't something she was proud of. Or even understood.

They were both silent.

"Does He do things for you? When you pray?" Clay finally asked.

He sounded skeptical and Rene could see where this was going.

"You can't blame Him. I know the smart thing for me would have been to keep working at the café until I saved enough to pay for any complications on this trip." Rene didn't want to talk about her finances, but she wanted to talk about her relationship with God even less. "I never have been good with money."

Clay shrugged.

"It's just—" Rene said and then paused. So many other emotions had gone wrong for her lately that she wanted to get this one right. "Have you ever felt like life was passing you by and you needed to do something different—even *be* something different—before it was too late and you missed your one true destiny?"

Clay must have been surprised at the question, because he tilted his head up again so she could see his eyes once more. "I'm not much into destiny. But sure, I've felt a need to change. The last time I sat a bronc. That's why I quit."

Rene had wondered why he left the rodeo, but she could see by the set to his chin that he wasn't going to say any more on the topic. He was looking at her like he expected an answer, though.

"Well, mine wasn't quite that dramatic," she said. "I mean, the one before this stuff with Trace."

No one spoke for a minute.

"It was your mother, wasn't it?" Clay asked softly.

Rene nodded. She'd spent years postponing her life while she took care of her invalid mother. She'd told Clay all about it. "Not that I ever regretted taking care of her. It's just after she was gone, I looked around and what did I have left?"

Rene swallowed. Her mother had been bed-ridden, but she was only in her fifties. She was supposed to live for many more years. Rene had been stunned when she died. God had not only refused to answer Rene's prayers for her mother's healing, but He had turned His back on her when she needed Him the most. It's like He had just walked out of the room when her mother died.

"You have your cousin and that artist aunt of yours. That's more than some people have." Clay said.

Rene looked up. Clay didn't talk much, so she was amazed at how often he managed to say the right thing when he did speak. "Thanks."

She ate another bite of her hamburger and refused to dwell on how much she missed her mother. She'd be in tears again if she did.

Instead, she turned to Clay. "You never did tell me about your mother."

"There's nothing to tell."

If Rene had a dime for all of the questions Clay had refused to answer on the ride up here, she could have bought her own tow truck by now. "Well, you can at least tell me if she's still living or not."

"No, I can't. I have no idea."

"Oh, I'm—"

"Don't say you're sorry," Clay warned. His eyes smoldered as he turned to look at her. "I'm long past the time of needing a mother."

Rene set her hamburger down. She couldn't help herself. She reached over and touched Clay's arm. "I'm sorry anyway."

Rene drew her hand back quickly. She wasn't altogether comfortable with this man and she wondered if she'd stepped over some invisible line. Sympathy seemed to make him nervous. Then his lips twisted in a small smile and she relaxed.

"You remind me of her, you know," he said.

"I do?" Rene blinked back a tear. "Why that's the nicest thing anyone has said to me since—"

Clay shook his head and turned to face the front of the cab. "No, it's not. Nice, I mean. She stopped coming to see me at the foster care place when I was seven. My dad had been dead for years. The social services people couldn't even find her to ask if she'd give me up for adoption. And, believe me, they tried."

Rene completely forgot about her own grief. The sky had grown darker as they had been sitting here so the truck was filled with shadows. She didn't need to see Clay's face, though, to know his whole body was tense. "That must have been terrible. I would *never* do something like that. I can imagine how you must have felt."

"I felt just fine," he said with a hard edge to his voice.

"I—" Rene began. His profile was stern.

"It's okay," he said in a softer voice as he turned to look at her and his face relaxed. "The foster care places weren't so bad. They suited me better than a regular adoption thing anyway because I got moved around a lot. I wasn't much into families. But I always had food and a place to stay. That's all I needed. I did fine."

"But where was your uncle?"

"My mother wasn't talking to him. He didn't know how to reach us. I didn't even know my mother had a brother until he showed up a few years ago."

Clay was still holding the last piece of his hamburger, his hand resting against the steering wheel. Rene didn't know what else to say that would help so she stayed quiet.

"You're sure this aunt of yours is expecting you?" Clay asked.

Rene nodded.

Aunt Glory had invited her and Paisley to help paint an art mural months ago. The work even paid. The first thing Rene had done when she decided to leave Texas was to phone her aunt and ask if the offer was still good.

"My cousin has probably called her again by now," Rene said brightly. She hadn't wanted her cousin to worry so she hadn't told her she was being towed to Dry Creek. "They'll both be wondering where I am."

Clay nodded.

"Finish up that burger before it gets cold," he said as he crumpled up the papers that had held his own food.

Rene took another bite. "I can't wait to get to Dry Creek."

Clay grunted and turned the ignition in his truck. "I just hope we beat the snow there."

Rene shrugged. "I don't think we need to worry too much about what the clerk said about the weather forecast."

"He got the information right off the television in the back room." Clay turned to look at her. "It sounded pretty solid to me."

"But it's almost April," Rene protested. "It can't snow like that now. Spring should be here soon."

Rene figured the weather, at least, needed to act like it was supposed to act. The rest of her world was tilting. Some things needed to stay steady on their axes.

Just then she saw a snowflake fall on the windshield. It appeared as though God wasn't going to give them any breaks on this trip. But then that shouldn't surprise her. That's how her life had been going lately.

Chapter Two

"I can't believe it's still snowing like this," Rene whispered. They were parked in the middle of the one street in Dry Creek, Montana. It was past midnight and thick wet flakes filled the black night, landing softly on the windshield of the truck. "My aunt said to just ask anyone for directions to her house, but—"

Rene hadn't realized the town was so very tiny. Because her mother couldn't travel, Aunt Glory had always visited them at their home in Rosemead, California, instead of inviting them to Dry Creek.

The snow was falling so fast Rene could barely see the buildings on either side of the one street. The lone streetlight glowed in the darkness, but all it showed were some parked cars half-buried in the snow. She'd seen abandoned buildings in Los Angeles that showed more signs of life than this little town.

"There must be other houses somewhere," Rene said as she looked around in bewilderment. "I count—what—seventeen? And that looks like a café. And that one's a store of some kind. Can this even add up to a town?"

"It does in this part of Montana," Clay said. He was glad to see Rene's face lit up with interest as she looked around. "I've seen towns with less in the Dakotas."

"Well, at least we shouldn't have any trouble finding my aunt," Rene said. She could see the white puffs she and Clay made with each breath. "If we don't freeze to death first."

"A blizzard always looks worse in the night," Clay said. "We could just knock on one of the doors and ask where your aunt is. Everyone would know in a town like this."

They'd driven straight through from their stop at the fast-food place. The roads had gotten worse with each hour that passed.

"I suppose." Rene crossed her arms in an effort to get warmer. Neither one of them made any move to open the doors of the tow truck. Rene knew it was more than just figuring out which house to go to that was holding her back. She was puzzled by something. After she'd eaten that hamburger, the night had become enchanted.

It almost felt like she and Clay were in the middle of a snow globe that someone had turned upside down. She'd even felt faint a time or two when she looked over at Clay as he drove. His profile intrigued her in the night. Before her lesson with Trace, she might have thought that meant she and Clay had the beginnings of a grand love affair.

Now, she had to conclude that it was just the natural effects of the cold and her lack of sleep. Granted, there had been something cozy about traveling north with this man in his tow truck, but he was just doing his job. He didn't even talk like he believed in love.

Rene might be disappointed in love, but she still knew it existed for other people. She looked over at Clay.

"I'll send you the first money I get—" she swallowed. It suddenly occurred to her that no one would be working on the mural in this kind of weather. She hadn't mentioned to Clay that the mural was going to be painted on the outside of a barn. "It might take a little bit. I can sign an IOU or something for the bill."

"I haven't had a chance to figure it up yet."

Frost was starting to build a thin film on the windows of the cab.

"Well, when you do—" Rene stopped and leaned forward. "Is that a light over there?"

It was hard to see through the falling snow, but it did look to Rene like a beacon shone in the window of the small church down the street. That must be where her aunt's husband was the pastor. "I bet there's someone inside who can tell me where my aunt lives."

"Even if no one's there, it's probably warm. Maybe they put the lights on so anyone who needed to would feel welcome to go inside out of the storm."

Rene nodded. She didn't know much about blizzards, but she and Clay had driven over a few sections of highway that were covered with so much snow that a regular car wouldn't make it through. There might be other people out there who didn't have four-wheel drive or extra traction and they might need temporary shelter.

"Well, let's go see." Clay pushed his hat down farther on his head before he reached into the glove compartment and pulled out one of the flashlights. Rene pulled her windbreaker around her and reached for her own door handle.

"Let me come around before you leave the cab," Clay said as he opened his door.

If it wasn't for the glow of the flashlight, Rene would have lost sight of Clay in the darkness as he walked around the front of the truck.

"Wow," Rene said when Clay opened her door. The weak light from inside the cab partially lit up the outside. She could see that the snow was already two feet deep on the ground. The flakes sparkled like tiny diamonds. The light made Clay's face look softer, too. He stood outside her door for a second as though he, too, were caught up in the enchantment.

Then he swallowed and stopped looking at her.

"Here." Clay reached around to the small bench that formed the backseat of his truck. Then he pulled out a pair of tall rubber boots. "I use these for fishing, but they should keep your feet dry." Clay reached into the boots. "There should be some wool socks in here, too."

Clay pulled out a pair of long gray socks. There was a hole in the heel of one sock, but they both looked warm to Rene. It had been almost seventy degrees when she left Mule Hollow. She had some flimsy flats on her feet and no socks at all.

"Thank you," Rene said as she slipped her shoes off.

Clay had to clear his throat. He was having a hard time concentrating. Rene had delicate toes painted in a soft pink. The sight of them made his knees weak. Or maybe it was the cold that was affecting him. Her feet were beautiful, though; she even had a silver ring twisted around one toe.

He couldn't even remember if the socks were clean. He usually just threw the socks in the boots after a fishing trip and then washed them when he got a chance. He wasn't sure that chance had come since his last fishing trip. He couldn't ask her to put her bare feet in those boots, though. The rubber would be bitter cold against the snow.

Clay took off his gloves so he wouldn't accidentally touch her feet with the snow that had already fallen on the gloves. He could feel her shiver slightly as he held her bare feet in his hands. He knew he should put the socks on as quickly as he could, but he didn't. He allowed all of the warmth to leave his hands and go into her feet. Only then did he pull on the socks.

The temperature outside the truck must have been zero. It wasn't only her feet that would be cold. Clay reached behind the truck seat and pulled out a blanket. "Wrap this around yourself. That jacket of yours won't do much good."

Clay resisted the urge to kiss Rene on the forehead when she finally stepped down from the cab. She looked like a refugee with the blanket wrapped around her head and the rubber boots on her feet.

"Here. Careful that you don't slip," Clay said. After all of this, he hoped the church was not locked. He wasn't sure what churches did about locks in a small town like this. He'd never had much reason to go to church, so the rules were a mystery to him.

Clay dipped his hat so the snow wouldn't collect on top of it. "Walk in my footsteps as much as you can."

Rene slid down to the ground and Clay pulled the blanket tighter around her head.

"My hair—"

"Forget your hair. Here, take my gloves."

Clay slipped the gloves on Rene's hands before turning around and starting to walk toward the church.

Rene's blanket was white when they got to the steps of the church and Clay knew he must be covered with snow, too. His fingers were cold when he gripped the icy door handle and gave it a push.

"It's open." Rene's relief was obvious as she stepped through the door he held for her.

Clay felt the warm air as he stepped into the church. They were in a small entry hall and a couple of coats were hanging on the rack to their left. There was still snow on one of the coats so he figured whoever was inside the church hadn't been there for long. He was comforted to see a couple of well-worn Stetsons on the shelf above the coat rack. One of them even looked like it had been knocked to the ground as often as his. Which meant there must be some working ranchers inside here. Maybe even some horsemen. He trusted men like that.

Rene's cheeks were still pale from the cold, but she lowered the blanket and slipped her feet out of the rubber boots. The socks covered her feet.

Muffled sounds came from the main part of the church and Clay decided they might as well find out who else had sought the warmth of this place. They hung their coats and the blanket on the high rack.

"They're praying," Rene whispered as they walked into the large room with pews lining each side. There was a blue flannel banner hanging in the front that had a white dove angled downward on it.

Clay figured he would have known what the people were doing without Rene announcing it to him. But it was a strange time to be praying. It suddenly occurred to him that he hadn't seen any cars parked in front of the church, either, so these people must have walked here.

He wondered if he'd stumbled into some kind of a cult meeting. It wasn't natural for people to get up in the middle of the night—in a blizzard—and walk to a church and pray.

One thing was for sure. He was going to stay back here

in the shadows. Just going inside a church made him nervous enough without having any unusual behavior to deal with. He didn't want to see anyone crying hysterically. Or thinking they heard the voice of God. He saw no reason to talk to the people here, either. Any kind of religious outbursts would make him uneasy. He didn't even like the enthusiasm of Tupperware salesmen.

He glanced down at Rene. Her face was pinking up nicely.

The warm air made Rene's skin tingle. She hadn't seen her aunt since her mother's funeral, and the rich copper of Glory's hair was a little more subdued than it had been then. Not that Rene would ever fail to recognize her, even when her aunt sat on a pew facing the front of the church with a gray wool scarf half wrapped around her bowed head.

Although she couldn't hear the prayers, Rene bowed her head and joined with the others. Praying from the back of the church was enough for her.

A phone rang somewhere in one of the back rooms. Rene heard an "Amen" and the people in front turned around. An older man in overalls and a plaid shirt started walking down a side aisle, probably to answer the phone. A second man followed him.

Rene took a step closer to the front before her aunt turned her head and saw her.

"You made it!" Glory called out.

Rene told herself she should have come to Dry Creek sooner. Her aunt's round face glowed with joy as she braced a hand on the end of the pew and slowly rose, holding a wooden crutch in her other hand.

"What happened?" Rene hurried down the aisle.

Clay watched as Rene ran toward the middle-aged woman who had to be her aunt. He shifted slightly. He told himself he should feel good. He'd delivered Rene to her family. She was no longer his responsibility. He watched as she greeted the others at the front of the church. Somehow the relief he expected to feel didn't come surging up inside, though. All he could think about was that he needed to get his radio fixed before he made the long drive back to Mule Hollow.

If it wasn't so cold outside, Clay would have turned around and left the church. He should quietly unload Rene's car from his truck and leave it on the street. He could mail the bill once he got back to Mule Hollow. He didn't like goodbyes and he'd just as soon slip away before he had to say one to Rene. She might get all emotional and he'd just stand there feeling awkward. Or, worse yet, he'd end up stammering out something about how much he'd liked being with her on the drive up here. Yes, it was best to avoid that. He should go.

But the warm air kept coming from heating vents on the wall behind him and he figured it wouldn't hurt to stand in the church for little longer, at least until his toes stopped tingling. Besides, Uncle Prudy was always telling him that he needed to start doing some of the things that normal people did. Clay half-agreed with him; his days in the foster care system hadn't done much to show him what a regular life was like.

It had taken Clay years to admit there might be more to life than riding broncs. The rodeo world had felt natural to him, probably because he was always breaking camp and moving on to the next ride. Leaving is what he did best. Back then, he had been surrounded by men who lived the same kind of life. They were all buddies, but none of them were really friends.

After Uncle Prudy tracked him down, Clay had started wondering if he hadn't missed something by not having neighbors and friends and a place to put his socks that didn't change with each motel room. That's why, when his uncle mentioned the tow truck business, Clay agreed to try it. He wasn't sure it would work, but he had to take the chance just in case there was more to life.

It would make Uncle Prudy feel good to know he had stopped in a church.

Clay had become so comfortable leaning against the back wall that he wasn't paying as much attention as he normally would. Rene and her aunt were halfway down the aisle before he realized they were coming straight at him. Rather, the aunt was coming and Rene was following behind trying to get the other woman's attention. He looked around quick, but there was no escape. The woman looked determined and she was moving pretty fast for a woman with a crutch.

"You must be Rene's young man," the aunt said in a rush of words when she reached him. "I was sure there had been some misunderstanding and you'd come running after her. She's a wonderful woman. I'm glad you see that."

Clay listened in dismay until the woman finished. "I didn't—I mean, I do see, but—"

"He's not my boyfriend," Rene interrupted, with a look of horror on her face. She was out of breath and pinker than Clay had ever seen her. "He's the tow truck driver. My car had problems and—"

"Well." The other woman looked at Rene and then back at Clay. "Paisley didn't tell me about a tow truck man."

"I didn't want her to worry," Rene said quietly. "I'll call her tomorrow."

Clay was being inspected like a bug on the wall.

"I'm bonded," Clay offered. It didn't sound like much, but it was the best he could think to say. He was used to men taking his measure, but not the female relatives of young women he'd driven up from Texas.

"Of course," the woman finally said as her face relaxed into a smile. "And I see you wear a cross. We're so glad you brought our Rene to us."

Even though she leaned on a crutch, the older woman stretched one arm out like she planned to step forward and hug him.

Clay ducked his head and took off his hat. He should have taken the thing off earlier. "No need to thank me. And, the cross is not—"

"He's just doing his job," Rene whispered fiercely to her aunt. It didn't seem to matter, though.

Clay wished he could drop his hat to the floor and step on it so the tiny decoration was hidden. It was too late, though, because Rene's aunt was done studying him and was making that last step toward him.

In all the years that he'd ridden rodeo, Clay had never once closed his eyes during a ride, not even when he knew he'd soon be lying in the dust and aching all over. But he couldn't help himself; he closed his eyes when he felt the older woman's arms reach around and hug him.

Clay's hat fell out of his hand and he felt the crutch pressing into his ribs. He didn't think a hug should last this long. He hadn't saved someone's life or anything. It was just a tow truck job. He was even going to charge; maybe not the whole amount, but enough so it wouldn't be charity.

"I can't thank you enough," the woman said when she finally released him.

Clay took a deep breath.

"No problem," he managed to say, and then he tried to smile.

He got his lips to cooperate until he saw the older woman's face. He couldn't remember the last time someone had looked at him with such an expression of kindness, and he wasn't sure what to do. All he could think was that, if this was a cult, they sure did brainwash their people well. Rene's aunt looked delighted to see him.

Clay bent down to get his Stetson. The cross on his hat band was a beat-up old tie tack that had belonged to his father. Clay had worn it on his hats for so long, he'd almost forgotten it was there.

"Those roads are so bad out there, I thought Rene would be staying someplace waiting for the blizzard to be over," the older woman said quietly when he straightened back up. He shifted his hat in his hand so the cross was to the back. If he didn't think it would provoke more discussion, he would have taken the tie tack off and put it in his pocket.

"Clay's got a great tow truck." Rene was standing beside her aunt and talking with more energy than the subject warranted. "Some kind of special make for off-road driving. Has lots of horsepower."

"It gets me where I need to go." He wondered when he could make his move to leave. He didn't want Rene to feel she had to defend him or, worse yet, boost his ego.

Just then a man walked past Rene and looked at Clay. "Did I overhear that you're a tow truck driver?"

The man's voice was low and raspy; it almost sounded like he was sick.

Clay nodded cautiously. Middle-aged and sturdy, this was the man who had been leading the prayers earlier, so he must be Rene's uncle. The minister. Clay had never talked to a minister before. He was surprised that the guy looked so ordinary. Wearing a worn flannel shirt and jeans, he could almost be a rodeo rider. He did smell of menthol, though, and his face was flushed.

"What a relief," the man said as he held out his hand to Clay. "I'm not contagious, by the way. The doctor says I have an infection, so no one else should get it."

"I'm not worried." Clay put his hat back on his head before he reached out and shook the minister's hand. He figured that got him one step closer to leaving.

"I'm Matthew Curtis. Rene's uncle."

"Clay Preston."

The handshake was over and Clay glanced over at the door. "I—ah—"

Matthew coughed. "Don't leave yet. I just got a call and we have a car stuck east of here."

Rene's aunt leaned forward on her crutch. "But the snowplow's working the road to the west."

The man nodded. "That was the Miles City sheriff on the phone. He got a call about a family with a baby in some car. The connection didn't hold for long. Anyway, the sheriff wants us to send someone out right away. It's where County Road J crosses over. A little baby can get cold mighty fast, and we're a lot closer than Miles City."

Clay felt his muscles relax. He had an excuse to leave. "I'll go get them. My truck cuts through snow almost as good as a plow does."

The minister started beaming. "You're an answer to our prayers."

Clay felt his breath catch in his chest. He looked over at Rene. He couldn't tell what she thought, but she looked surprised. Well, so was he. People had called him some strange things in his day, but no one had ever called him an answer to prayer before, not even when they saw his hat.

"It's nothing. Anyone would do the same," Clay said. He hoped no one was going to hug him again.

"Maybe so, but none of us have a vehicle that can get through on a night like this. That's why we met here. We were trying to figure out what we would do if we did get a call and needed to send someone out."

"Well, I'll be happy to help," Clay told the man. He'd be able to slip away after he brought those people back from the cold. When he thought about it, he was glad he was here. Right now, those people needed his help a whole lot more than they needed God's.

Of course, it would not be respectful to tell the minister that. Clay didn't share the pastor's belief in a God who actually listened to people, but, like Rene's foolishness about love, he could understand how people would want these things to be true. Emotions, he'd noticed in his forty-one years, led people to believe some strange things. Look at him.

He believed that cross he pinned to his hat made him closer to the father he'd never met. His mother had given him the tie tack one day, almost throwing the thing at him while muttering that she didn't want anything that reminded her of the complete failure his father had been. Clay knew he himself was also a disappointment to his mother, so he held on to the tie tack as though it might someday show him what his father had done that was so wrong.

Chapter Three

Clay pulled his Stetson low on his face. If he had more time, he'd unload Rene's car before he left. But bringing in that family came first. Everything should be ready to go in a few minutes.

Midnight showed through the church windows, and low-wattage bulbs on the ceiling lit up Rene's face as she stood beside a pew sorting through a cardboard box of stray mittens. Some of the gloves were red. Some blue. Others were a rainbow of colors.

Apparently, people lost their belongings in churches just as often as they did at rodeos, Clay mused. There were more children's mittens in the box than he usually saw, but that was the only difference.

Rene had already apologized three times for the misunderstanding about him being her boyfriend. He could have avoided the last two apologies if her aunt and uncle hadn't decided they needed to find some food for the stranded family. The older couple had gone into the church kitchen and the two other men had gone into one of the rooms to draw a map showing the gravel road to the east where the car was supposed to be. No one said Clay had to wait inside for everyone to finish, though. He had a perfectly good heater in his truck.

Clay felt like he should say something to Rene before he left the church, but he hesitated. The sight of her sorting through all of those little mittens made him want to stay. Which was completely foolish since, in her mind, he was only the tow truck guy. The fact that he was bothered by that is why he knew he needed to leave and wait outside. By the time he got back with the family, Rene should be in bed at her aunt's house.

"Look at these." Rene held up two tiny mittens with delight on her face. She put the pink mittens on her thumbs like puppets and wiggled them.

"I didn't know babies wore mittens," Clay said and then he swallowed. Rene hadn't smiled like this since she left Mule Hollow. She glowed. His butterfly woman was back. He had to admit it made him feel good to see it until he realized it was mittens that had made her smile and not him.

"I'll set them aside for the baby," Rene said as she slipped the tiny mittens off her thumbs and put them in the pocket of the heavy coat she had borrowed from her aunt. "The poor thing. What a night to be out there stuck."

Rene's blond hair swirled around her when she moved. Clay could almost imagine sliding his hands down the smooth locks of her hair and then dipping her head back a little so he could—

"You might want to get some blankets ready, too," Clay interrupted himself. Those kinds of thoughts did no one any good, least of all him. "It wouldn't hurt to warm the blankets in the oven after I leave, either, so they'll be ready."

Clay ran his hand over his chin and felt the stubble on his face. He wished he'd pulled off the road yesterday and shaved. Just because he was here doing a job, it didn't mean he couldn't look better.

"I'll let my aunt know," Rene said and looked back down into the box. "I need a scarf, too. Your truck is warm enough inside, but we'll probably need to go out when we get to the car that's stuck."

"What?" Clay frowned. Had he heard right? This wasn't part of the plan. "I thought you were staying here with your aunt. Where it's warm."

Clay didn't mind doing a rescue mission in a snowstorm, but he sure didn't want to take Rene with him. He knew women were strong and capable, but they might need to dig the car out of a snowbank, and he didn't want Rene outside shivering in a blizzard. Not when he could spare her that.

Just then Rene's aunt and uncle came back from the kitchen.

"We've got blankets and some warm milk," Rene's aunt said as she pointed to the thermos her husband was setting on the pew next to the mitten box. "Hopefully, the mother has an empty bottle for the baby."

Rene was still staring at Clay. "You can't go after them alone."

"Alone?" The minister straightened up and looked at Clay, too. "Of course, you can't go alone. I don't know what we were thinking. I'll just take a double dose of my medicine and—"

"You'll do no such thing," his wife interrupted him. "The doctor said you needed to take care of yourself. You shouldn't even be over here tonight. I'll just wrap my ankle a little better and—"

"Neither one of you are going," Rene said firmly. "I'm all dressed for the cold. I'm the logical one to go. I'm happy to go."

"But I don't need anyone to come," Clay protested as he slid a step closer to the door.

"That's not—" The minister turned at a sound from the hallway. "Here come Charlie and Elmer now. We'll all pray over the two of you before you go."

"I don't think we need—" Clay began.

Rene shot him a look as the two older men entered the room, and then she said, "We'd be grateful for all the prayers we can get."

Rene reached over and put her hand on Clay's arm.

"I'm going," she said. "If you're worried about having enough room, I'll sit in the backseat after you pick up the family. But you're not going alone."

Clay was speechless. He gave up. Prayer. No prayer. Company. No company. It didn't matter. He would take the whole bunch of them if they wanted. He needed to hurry. He told himself it was because of the baby out in that car, but he knew it was as much for his own sake.

No one had ever cared if he went someplace alone before. He'd never had anyone pray over him, either. It made him feel a little uncomfortable. He'd had his leg broken from a fall on his first bronc, and no one had offered to pray over him back then or keep him company at the doctor's office. He supposed a prayer couldn't hurt a person, though, even if these old men were putting their hands on his shoulder.

Clay noticed Rene had closed her eyes and didn't look worried.

"Father, protect our friends here as they get that family

out of the snow." One of the older men was speaking. "We know You control the weather and that You watch over each of us. We put Clay and Rene in Your hands and we ask for Your mercy on our worried friends out there in the storm. Keep them safe. Amen."

Clay opened his eyes. He hadn't been planning to close them all of the way, but midway through the prayer he started to feel peaceful. This praying business did seem to have some psychological effect. Maybe that's how the church got people to join up with them. Maybe they sedated them with prayer and then got them to say okay.

"Well, we best get going," Clay said. The more he thought about it, the more he realized that that peaceful feeling must be a delayed reaction to the snow. That made more sense than the prayers. It was bitter cold outside and it was still affecting him.

Clay picked up the thermos and the blankets and the minister opened the church door for him. He drew his breath in. The wind bit more sharply than it had earlier. And the snow was deeper on the ground. All of the footsteps they had made coming to the church were now covered with snow.

Rene walked behind Clay on the way back to his truck so she could step in the tracks he made. She wasn't sure, but she thought he was taking shorter steps so he would match her stride better.

"I can keep up," she said. The wind blew her words back in her face, though, and she didn't think Clay even heard what she said. "You don't need to slow down for me."

She had listened to enough blizzard stories from Aunt Glory to know that people could die when it was twenty degrees below zero outside. She trusted Clay to be able to bring the people in safely. But she knew she could help, too.

Rene was glad she had her mittens when Clay opened the passenger door and she steadied herself on the side of the truck so she could climb up into the seat. Even with the mittens, the cold steel of the metal chilled her skin. The dim overhead light gave a white glow to the inside of the cab. Snow had covered the windshield when they had been inside the church.

Clay stopped to wipe off the snow after he closed her door. Even with the snow gone, she could barely see him as he walked around to the driver's door.

"You okay?" Clay asked as he climbed up into the seat and closed his door.

Rene nodded. She didn't want to say anything because she thought her teeth might chatter. Clay had a fine layer of snow on his hat and she could feel the snow in her hair.

Clay turned the ignition and the heater started up at the same time.

"It'll take a minute before the air will blow warm," Clay said as he put the truck into reverse and started to back up. "Unfortunately, we don't have time to wait."

"Of course, we can't wait," Rene agreed. She lifted the mittens to her face and blew warm air on them before sliding them along her cheeks. "I would never expect someone to spend time warming the cab up for me when a family is stuck in a blizzard."

What kind of a person did he think she was? Was that why he hadn't wanted her to come with him? She knew she'd been a little preoccupied with her own problems on the ride up here, but when it came to life and death— "I'm good in emergencies."

Clay shifted into four-wheel drive and headed east. He'd

taken his gloves off before he started his truck and he felt the cold of the steering wheel in his hands. He could hear the hurt in Rene's voice and he was sorry he'd put it there.

"I'm sure you are," he said, hoping he had enough encouragement in his voice. "You remembered the milk. That's going to be a big help."

"My aunt is the one who thought of heating up some milk."

"But you carried it out here," Clay said. He sounded like an idiot. If he needed any more proof that he shouldn't even be talking to an emotional woman, this was it. He was the proverbial bull in a china shop. Fortunately, Rene seemed willing to let the whole thing be.

Which was good because he needed to concentrate on what little bit of the road he could see. The old men had drawn him a map and it was lying on top of the blankets next to him. There wasn't much to the map, though. Mostly it was a curved line going east with a couple of local ranches marked. If it wasn't for the barbed wire fences on both sides of the road he wouldn't even know where he should be driving. It was dark and the snowdrifts were already up to the bottom wire on the fences.

"I thought my aunt said there were ditches along the road," Rene said after they'd been driving for a bit.

Clay nodded. "They're there, all right. We just can't see them because the snow has filled them in."

What he left unsaid was causing him to grip the steering wheel and peer into the darkness on either side of his truck's high beams. Because he couldn't see these side ditches, it increased the chance that he'd drive off course and end up in one of them. When he'd said his tow truck would go anywhere in a blizzard, he'd forgotten how much of Montana was covered with narrow gravel roads lined with wide ditches.

The night was silent. Everything that could scurry in this countryside had already squeezed into its burrow or was huddled behind some bush. Also, the winds had died down and, while the snow still fell quietly, it came down thick and wet, muffling any other sounds.

"I think I see a light," Rene said as she leaned forward in her seat. "Off to the left—no—" Rene looked for another minute and then fell back to her seat. "I guess it was nothing."

"It's easy to see things that aren't here in this kind of weather," Clay said.

"Wishful thinking, I guess," Rene said.

"Or maybe the clouds parted and it's the moon reflecting off of something," Clay said. "The important thing is to look at the map and go by what it says. It's not good to trust anything but a map in these kinds of conditions."

"I usually don't use a map," Rene admitted.

"Tonight's no time for guessing," Clay said.

Clay saw Rene pick up the paper map from the seat beside him.

"If you need a flashlight, there's one in the glove compartment," he told her. "Use the little one. The big one will be too bright. I keep that for distances."

Rene took out the small flashlight and shined it on the map. "It doesn't look like there are any ranch houses off to that side."

Clay saw a cluster of trees near a crossroads ahead.

"This should be on the map," Clay said, nodded his head toward the road that intersected the one they were on.

"It is," Rene said as she pointed to a spot on the map.

"It says it's County Road J. That's the road they mentioned. And the car is supposed to be stuck on the other side of it."

Rene let the map fall to her lap and she leaned forward. "I don't see anything yet, though. Do you?"

Clay shook his head. "Not yet."

Rene kept looking for a minute and then she turned to him. "You don't think there's any chance we'll miss them, do you?"

Clay had hoped that possibility wouldn't occur to her. He tried to keep the worry out of his voice. "We should be fine if the map is accurate. And the sheriff got it right when he talked to them."

Fortunately, Rene didn't ask any more questions. It had occurred to Clay earlier that they were relying heavily on a cell phone conversation that hadn't been clear and the assumptions of a man in the sheriff's office who might have his directions scrambled, given the number of cars that were stuck to the west of Dry Creek.

"Is that it?" Rene said as she pointed ahead.

It was so dark that Clay could barely make out the snow-covered mound in the distance. "I hope so."

He had expected to see a trail of exhaust coming from the vehicle. A man from these parts would know to keep the snow swept away from the exhaust while he kept the engine going with its heater. No one had kept the snow away from that car, though. "It might be a car that's abandoned."

"Maybe someone else came along and picked them up," Rene said as she leaned forward.

Clay didn't answer. Nothing had come down this road lately except his truck. Even if the tracks were filled in, the snow would have drifted differently after it had been disturbed. Maybe a vehicle had come from the other direction and then gone back that same direction, but that was not likely. According to the hand-drawn map, Dry Creek was the nearest town or ranch. Anyone rescuing that family would have taken them there.

Clay hoped he was missing some logical explanation for what they saw.

The truck's headlights shone on the snow-covered car and Clay slowed as he came closer. The car was jackknifed in the road, so he could not drive past it, not even if he wanted to. None of the windows were wiped clear of snow, and he'd have to shovel snow away from the doors before he could open them.

He rolled down his window.

"Hello there," he called.

He listened, but he couldn't hear an answer from inside the car.

"Someone must have picked them up already," Rene repeated herself as though she was trying to convince herself.

Clay heard the worry in her voice. It was the same worry he felt. The family would be very cold if they were inside that car.

He switched the engine off. "There's no point in both of us going out in the snow."

Clay was glad when Rene nodded and didn't argue with him. He opened his door and then turned to look back at Rene. He wanted to say something to ease her worry. "You know, it wouldn't hurt to pray."

He did not wait for her to answer before he stepped down from the cab. He wouldn't have thought it was possible for the night to get any colder, but it had.

Chapter Four

Rene watched as Clay walked toward the half-buried car. The truck lights were off and she had to strain to see him through the dark of the night. He'd grabbed a shovel from the back of his truck and, within minutes, was bending to scoop up the snow, clearing it from the driver's-side door.

"Please, Lord, let them be safe," Rene whispered in the stillness. *Listen to me, listen to me,* she pleaded silently.

There was a bitter chill in the air from when Clay had opened his door. She wished there was something more she could do for the family. Suddenly, she realized there was. She unbuttoned her coat and pulled the top blanket next to her before wrapping her coat back around her. At least one of the blankets would be warm in case the baby needed it. The small flashlight Clay had used earlier was on the seat, too, and she slipped that into her pocket.

The window was starting to film over and she used her mittens to wipe it clear. Thankfully, she could still see Clay's shape as he worked. Finally, he set the shovel against the side of the car. It looked to Rene like he had cleared enough snow for the door to open.

"Please, Lord," she added as Clay reached for the door handle. She kept willing God to hear her even as her fears rose. It had been the same when she'd prayed for her mother's healing. She kept praying as the news from the doctors worsened. She had faith right up until the last wrenching moment. Then she had nothing.

Rene waited for Clay to turn and wave at her, letting her know that the car was empty. Instead, he bent down and crawled inside the car. Rene rolled down her window just a little so she could call out to Clay and ask him what he saw. She didn't get any words formed before she heard a woman's frantic scream.

Rene opened the door and climbed to the ground. Something was wrong inside that car.

Clay told himself he should have brought the flashlight with him. There was no light in the car. If he hadn't been so worried, he would have thought about that.

"It's okay," he said softly into the blackness. "I'm here to help."

The woman must have been in the backseat of the car because Clay couldn't see anyone in the front. Even if the night hadn't been so dark, the snow covering the car was so thick it would have blocked light from reaching the inside. Everyone back there must be terrified. He could see the dim shape of a bundle of blankets. She must be wrapped up in them.

"Are you okay?" Clay asked. He strained his eyes looking for other shapes, but he didn't see any.

He was listening to the woman's rapid breathing when he heard the door on the truck close. He moved to the edge of the seat so he could warn Rene to speak quietly.

He could barely see Rene walking toward him. He didn't need to say anything to her about not yelling. She was already humming some kind of a song. He could hear the woman's breathing start to calm at the sound so he moved farther into the car to let Rene enter also.

Rene slid into the front seat.

"Lullabies always make me feel better, too," Rene said softly as she looked into the backseat. "Are you all right?"

"He's your husband?" the woman asked hesitantly. Her voice sounded young and scared. "He's not a bad man?"

Clay held his breath. He didn't expect Rene to lie, but it would be helpful if the woman trusted him. Marriage always seemed to make a man look safer to women. Since he needed to bring this woman and everyone else out of here, it would be easier if she wasn't afraid of him.

"I'll show you," Rene said and soon there was a beam from a flashlight directed outside of the car. The strong part of the beam hit the snow, but enough light filled the inside of the car so the woman in the backseat could see them.

Clay reached up to tip his hat back. Rene knew what she was doing. Too much light would have made it impossible for the woman to see. The backseat was still dark. But in the half-light he could see Rene's face and she was smiling sweetly enough to reassure anyone.

"He is a cowboy?" The woman's tentative voice came from the backseat.

"He used to ride in the rodeo," Rene announced, and Clay thought he heard some pride in her voice. "Won a lot of times, too. He's a strong man. You can trust him. I do."

Clay had to remind himself that Rene was only saying these things to put the woman at ease.

"I need—ahh—" The moan that interrupted the woman's comment was sharp and deep.

"Are you okay?" Rene asked as she moved the flashlight up higher.

Clay could finally really see into the backseat. A young woman—he didn't think she was more than seventeen years old—was leaning against the door. The bottom half of her face was wrapped in a brown scarf, and the rest of her face was pale except for a scattering of dark freckles. She had blankets over her and a coat on top of that. All of the muscles in her face looked tight as though she were bracing herself for another shooting pain. He knew she was cold, but that should not be doing this to her.

Clay looked away from her to search the rest of the car once again. The most alarming thing to him was the people who were not there. There was also supposed to be a man and a baby. "Where's your husband?"

"He went for help," the young woman said, taking shallow breaths again. "The baby—"

Surely the man didn't take the baby with him, Clay thought. Not even a fool would—and then it dawned on him. "You're not? I mean—the baby—"

He looked at the roundness of the woman's waist. At first, he thought it was just the way the blankets were bunched around her. Then he looked over at Rene. He saw the alarm rising on her face, too.

Whoa, Clay thought. This changed everything.

"You're not having a baby, are you?" Rene finally asked. "I mean *now*."

The woman moaned again. "No, I told my Davy no. Not now. The pains are just worry pains. I'm not due for weeks. He didn't need to go for help." She looked at Clay directly for the first time. "You need to find him. Please, I told him he shouldn't go, but he wouldn't listen. He's a stubborn guy. We argued and I said awful things."

Clay didn't blame the man for trying to get help. Anyone looking at the pregnant woman could tell she was in distress. A tear trickled down her face.

"Where was he going?" Clay asked, keeping his voice as calm as possible. Maybe the man knew this country and there was a farmhouse that wasn't on the map Clay had been given.

"He thought he saw some light," the woman said as she pointed to the east.

"How long ago did he leave?" Clay asked.

"Not long. I don't know, but not long."

"And a house?" Rene said softly. "Did he see a house?"

Clay was glad Rene was not scaring the pregnant woman by asking those questions with the urgency she must feel inside.

"He thought so, yes." The teenager's breath started to come more rapidly again. "You don't think he "

"Clay can find him," Rene said quickly. "Just take a few deep breaths and relax. You can trust Clay."

Clay opened his mouth and shut it again. Rene had to know he couldn't find a house if none was there.

"First, we need to move you into my truck," Clay said to the young woman. "I'll have to shovel some snow away from this back door so we can get you out of this car. Just stay where you are and—" Clay looked around for inspiration.

"Well, talk to me, of course," Rene added brightly. "I want to know all about this baby you're expecting. Do you know if it's a boy or a girl? Do you have names picked out? I've always liked old-fashioned names."

Clay recognized Rene's chatty waitress voice. It was just what they needed.

Clay waited for Rene to slide out of the car so he could move past her. It wouldn't take him more than a couple of minutes to get the snow cleared and then he could open the back door and carry the woman to his truck. He'd feel better once they had her back at Dry Creek where someone would know if she needed to go to the hospital.

Once he was outside of the car, Clay picked up his shovel and began to dig. He moved one shovelful of snow and then another. He wasn't so sure how this night was going to end.

Rene could hear the sounds of Clay digging up the snow. She'd left the door open because there was no point in closing it. The air was as cold inside as it was outside.

It felt like an eternity had passed since she'd given her hand to Mandy to hold. That was the young woman's name. Mandy Smith. She had grown up in Minneapolis and was moving with her Davy to some small town in Idaho. He had work there.

"Where are you and your husband traveling to?" Mandy asked after a bit.

Rene gave the other woman's hand a gentle squeeze. "We're not really married."

"Oh," Mandy said and her voice lowered. "We haven't been telling people, but Davy hasn't married me yet, either. He wants to wait until we get to our new home. You're not pregnant, are you? It's hard when you're pregnant."

"Oh," Rene said then stopped herself. Now was not the time to list her worries about a man who wanted to wait to marry his pregnant girlfriend. "The thing is, Clay and I are just traveling together. We're not—that is—"

Rene couldn't hear the sounds of the shovel anymore.

"She's paying me," Clay said from just outside the door.

"To tow my car," Rene clarified. If she didn't know better, she would think Clay was teasing her. Maybe he was just trying to put Mandy at ease. It can't have been easy for her to tell them that she wasn't married. Rene didn't want to make a big deal about it, though. "Clay owns this tow truck and he was taking me to Dry Creek. It's strictly business."

"We were planning to stop at Dry Creek for dinner," Mandy said wistfully. "I heard some truckers in North Dakota saying they've got some really good hamburgers in the café there. Good pie, too. Blueberry."

"If you're hungry, we have some warm milk," Rene offered.

"It's in the truck," Clay said as he reached out and opened the back car door. "That's where I'm taking you— so if you can, just slide yourself over here."

Clay counted the little gasps Mandy made as she slid across the backseat toward the door he'd just opened. He wished he knew what her breathing meant.

The young woman made it to the open door so Clay could bend down and lift her up in his arms. Rene reached up and wrapped the blankets more securely around her. The snow had stopped blowing as much, but Rene still draped a corner of the blanket over Mandy's face to keep it warm.

Rene was holding the flashlight so Clay could see clearly to walk. He had to admit, she had been right earlier when she'd said she was good in emergencies. He was surprised, but grateful. When he got to the truck, Rene stepped in front of him to open the passenger-side door. There would be plenty of room for the three of them on the main seat.

Clay set Mandy on the seat and let go of her. "Don't worry. We'll get you to a doctor."

"No," she gasped. "You have to find Davy first. He'll be worried if he comes back and I'm not here. We can't leave until—".

Clay wished he knew more about birthing babies. Just enough so he'd know how much time they had. No baby deserved to be born in the cab of a tow truck. But then Mandy had said she was weeks away from her delivery date.

Clay reached up and flipped on his cab's overhead light. The young woman looked almost feverish.

"Please." Mandy reached out her hand to Clay. "He's the father of my baby. I love him."

This, Clay thought to himself suddenly, is what Uncle Prudy was so set on teaching him. The look in Mandy's eyes was more than any man deserved, especially one who hadn't even married her yet. Clay felt a sudden stab of envy for the man who inspired that kind of love, though.

"I can only look for five minutes," Clay compromised with his common sense. "I'll take my high-beam flashlight and flash it in the direction he went. I might pick up something."

It would take a miracle for the man to see the flashlight. Clay knew that, but it was enough action to give everyone some hope. He reached over to open the glove compartment.

"You're sure you'll be okay?" Rene asked him.

Clay looked down at her. She still held the smaller flashlight pointed to the ground at his feet, but it gave enough light so he could see her eyes. She might not be looking at him with love, but there was certainly concern in her eyes. He supposed that was something.

"I won't be long," Clay said.

"Wait," the woman inside the truck demanded, her voice strained.

Clay and Rene both looked at her.

"You can't leave without kissing each other," Mandy said. She sounded a little frantic. "My Davy and I didn't kiss. And now he's out there lost and I didn't even kiss him goodbye."

"But—" Rene protested. "We aren't. I mean—"

Clay saw Rene's cheeks pink up and he felt a wistfulness he had no right to even acknowledge.

Sometimes, he told himself, a man lived his whole life without a drop of grace and then—just when he least expected it—the universe suddenly opened up and dropped a golden opportunity right into his hands. This was that moment.

"We don't want her to worry," Clay whispered as he stepped closer and cupped Rene's face with his hands. He knew his fingers were rough and cold, but he traced the line of her jaw anyway. Her skin was soft. And she wasn't pulling away—although that might be because she was in shock.

He forced himself to be still for a moment so she could pull back if she wanted. Her eyes grew wide, but she stayed steady. The snow continued to swirl around them, but Clay didn't mind. She probably expected him to give her one of those quick kisses on the cheek, just to satisfy Mandy. But Clay knew the odds. He'd never have a chance like this again.

Clay knew he'd made a mistake the minute his lips touched Rene's. He'd kissed hundreds of women, but it was never like this. His feet were frozen, but that didn't stop his lips from heating up. He wasn't doing very well in the breathing department, either. He needed to stop kissing her, but not as much as he needed to continue.

"That's how I should have kissed Davy. I just—ahhh—" Mandy moaned again.

Clay couldn't move, but Rene pulled away from him at the sound of the other woman's distress. The cold air blew on Clay's face and he blinked. His time in the sun was over. He was almost surprised to find he was still standing on this deserted road in the middle of a Montana blizzard.

"I need to make that search." Clay was relieved his voice still worked. But since it did, he checked to see that he had the flashlight in his hand. What had he done?

Rene was already turned away from him, talking softly to Mandy. He wished he could tell by the curve of her back how she felt about that kiss. Obviously, she wasn't as shaken by it as he was, since she had already turned her attention to someone else.

"I'll be back in a few minutes," Clay said, and he fled to the safety of the darkness. He needed some time to collect himself. He wondered if all of those hours spent with Rene in the truck were taking their toll on him. He prided himself on being level-headed. He only got emotional at rodeos and football games. He never thought a kiss would take hold of his insides and not let go.

A few minutes in the cold air was what he needed, Clay told himself as he walked across the shallow ditch and lifted up the middle strand of the barbed-wire fence. He bent down and stepped through the fence. It wasn't his feelings that he was worried most about. It was the rest of it that was troublesome. He'd seen enough of life to know there were no fairy-tale endings. Not in his life.

His feelings would eventually burn themselves out. But the disappointment could haunt him for life.

Chapter Five

Rene tried not to look at the bright light off to the side of the truck. Clay was slowly moving the flashlight in an arc, searching the area where Mandy said her boyfriend had gone. While Clay was doing that, Rene was trying to distract Mandy. They'd already exhausted the topic of what they'd eat when they got to Dry Creek.

They were quiet for a few seconds and then Mandy shifted around on the seat.

"Never let your man go off by himself in a snowstorm," she finally said. The inside of the cab was dark except for a small light on the ceiling. The heater was on and it was warming up nicely. "I should have stopped my Davy."

"I doubt you could have," Rene said as she opened her left arm to hug the young woman. "Not if he thought you needed help. Here. Put your head on me. You may as well stretch out as much as you can until Clay gets back."

Mandy put her head on Rene's shoulder. "He's going to marry you someday, you know."

"Who?" Rene adjusted the blankets as Mandy stretched out her legs.

"A rodeo man would make a good husband," Mandy muttered as she turned slightly and arched her back.

"Clay? He doesn't even believe in love."

Well, that got Mandy's attention, Rene thought as the younger woman looked up at her and frowned. "Really?"

Rene nodded.

"Well, you have to have love," Mandy said firmly. "Even my Davy says he loves me. It's important."

"I know." Rene wondered how her life had ever gotten so turned around. A few days ago she thought Trace was her destiny, and now she was kissing a man who would rather order up a wife from some catalog than actually fall in love. She'd felt the kiss he'd given her more deeply than she should, too. Which meant she needed to get back on track.

"I'm going to make a list," Rene said, "of all the things I need in a husband. That's how I'll know when I find the right one."

Mandy drew in her breath. "I can help. For you, not for me. I want my Davy."

Rene looked out the side window and saw that the light was coming back to the truck. She motioned for Mandy to sit up again. She doubted Clay had found Mandy's boyfriend. She'd have to keep the young woman distracted for a little bit more.

Clay took his hat off before he opened the door to his truck. Then he brushed his coat before climbing inside. He didn't want to scatter snow all over the women.

"Did you see him?" Mandy asked quietly from the middle of the seat.

Clay shook his head. "I'll need to come back."

"But—" Mandy protested until another pain caught her and she drew in her breath.

"It won't take long to get you to Dry Creek," Clay said as he started his truck. "Then I can come back and look some more."

Clay didn't like leaving the man out there any more than Mandy did, but it could take hours to find him, and the sooner they got Mandy comfortable and relaxed the sooner those pains of hers would go away.

"I feel a lot better," Mandy said. "If you'd just go back and look some more, I'll be fine."

Clay looked at the young woman as she bit her bottom lip. Mandy was in obvious pain regardless of what she said. "You're not fine, and there's no use pretending."

Mandy gasped, half in indignation this time.

Those pains worried Clay, but he assumed she must know the difference between the ones she was having and ones that signaled the baby was coming. Women went to class for that kind of thing these days. She probably just needed to lie down somewhere and put her feet up.

"He's right," Rene said as she put her hand on Mandy's stomach. "Davy wouldn't want you out here. He'll tell you that when we find him. And think of the baby."

Mandy turned to look at Rene and then back at Clay.

"You promise you'll come back?" Mandy asked. "Right away?"

"You have my word," Clay said. He'd need to turn around using that country road.

"That should be on your list," Mandy said as she looked up at Rene. "Number one—he needs to keep his word."

Clay wondered if the two women were still talking about the baby Mandy was having. It seemed a bit premature to worry about the little guy's character, but he was glad to see that the young woman had something to occupy her mind. Maybe she had plans for her baby to grow up to be president or something.

"I don't know," Rene muttered. "We can talk about it later."

"We've got some time," Clay said. "It'll take us fifteen minutes at least to get to Dry Creek. You may as well make your list."

Mandy shifted on the seat again. "So, you think trust is important in a husband?"

"A *husband?*" Clay almost missed the turn. "You're making a list for a husband?"

"Well, not for me," Mandy said patiently. She looked at him like he was slow. "It's Rene's list, of course."

Clay grunted. Of course.

"He should be handsome, too," Mandy added as she stretched. "But maybe not smooth, if you know what I mean. Rugged, like a man, but nice."

Clay could feel Mandy's eyes on him.

"I don't really think I need a list," Rene said so low Clay could barely hear her. She was huddled against the far door again.

Clay didn't know why he was so annoyed that Rene was making a list. "Just don't put Trace's name on that thing."

"I'm not going to put anyone's name on it," Rene said as she sat up straighter. "And you are the one who doesn't think people should just fall in love. I'd think you would *like* a list."

Clay had to admit she had a point. He should be in favor of a list like that; it eliminated the feelings. It must be all this stress that was making him short-tempered. "If you're going to have a list, you might as well make the guy rich."

That should show he was able to join into the spirit of the thing.

"There's no need to ridicule—" Rene began.

"A good job does help," Mandy interrupted solemnly. "Especially when you start having babies. I'm hoping the job in Idaho pays well. We need a lot of things to set up our home."

"You should make a list of what you need for your house," Clay said encouragingly. Maybe the women would talk about clocks and chairs instead of husbands.

"I have a set of dishes in the trunk of the car," Mandy said. "I've been saving them for our first house together. I hope they haven't gotten broken."

Rene was getting a headache. She wondered if it was because of the cold or because Clay was being so irritating. He knew very well that she wasn't looking for a rich husband. He probably just said that because she couldn't pay her bills.

"You'll get your money," Rene said.

"Huh?" Mandy looked up at her.

"Clay. He'll get his money," Rene repeated. "For towing my car."

"I'm not worried," Clay said.

"You're really *charging* her?" Mandy stared at Clay like he'd admitted to kicking puppies. "I thought you were kidding earlier."

"Of course, he's charging me," Rene snapped. "I already said this was a business deal."

"Yes, but I thought—" Mandy stopped right there.

Rene decided the young woman had realized she should stop while she was ahead, and then Rene heard the gasp that followed.

She looked over Mandy's head and caught Clay's eye.

"I'm going as fast as I can," he assured her quickly before turning back to the road. "We can't be more than five minutes away."

Clay had his hat pulled low over his face and he was leaning forward like he could urge his truck through the snow faster. The headlights cut through the night and showed the tracks they had made on the way here.

"When we get there, pull right up to the church door," Rene said to him. "They'll still be there praying, and we can find out where to take her."

Rene wondered where pregnant women went in Dry Creek. She didn't know if they had a doctor around. Her aunt might know something about childbirth, but Rene had never asked her. It wasn't the sort of thing that came up in their phone conversations.

Everyone was quiet until they saw the first house that marked the entrance into Dry Creek.

"We're here." Rene felt a relief she hadn't since the first time they pulled into the town. Now, a dozen or so houses looked like lots of civilization. It was certainly better than being stuck out in the middle of nowhere with a pregnant woman and a man who sounded as bewildered about the whole process of giving birth as she was.

"There are still lights in the church," Clay added, his voice sounding as relieved as her own.

The church door opened almost as soon as we pulled the truck to a stop next to the front steps. Rene walked behind Clay as he and her uncle helped Mandy into the church. The temperature was still cold outside, but the wind had died down some so the snow wasn't blowing around. Aunt Glory stood at the open door, the light behind her streaming out into the darkness.

Rene closed the door behind them. Mandy's face was pinched from the strain of walking, even with the two men helping her. Rene unwound the scarf around Mandy's head.

"Is there someplace she can lie down?" Clay asked. He was still holding Mandy up on one side.

It didn't take them more than a couple of minutes to get Mandy stretched out on the sofa in the pastor's study with her shoes on the floor and a cup of warm cocoa on a stand next to her.

Clay could feel the young woman's eyes on him as she lay on the sofa.

"I haven't forgotten," he said quietly as he stood up from where he'd knelt to take her shoes off. "I'm going to get some dry gloves and some rope. Then I'll go back."

"We'll want a thermos of coffee this time," Rene said as she headed to the door. "Or maybe tea. I'll fix something up."

Clay followed her out of the room. They were in the back hallway of the church and the light was dim.

"No," Clay said as he reached out to touch Rene on the shoulder. "I've got this one."

She turned around to face him. "We've already been through that. You can't go alone. It's not safe."

She was one stubborn woman, but Clay decided now was not the time to point that out to her. "I've got it covered."

The minister walked out of the door behind them and then closed it. "Conrad Nelson is coming over. He should be here any minute. You need someone who knows the area."

"If he can pinpoint the houses, that would help," Clay admitted. He had wondered if there was a way to get a more complete map. Davy wouldn't have had a chance to walk far, but he obviously couldn't see the flashlight Clay had swung around earlier.

"There are no houses out where you picked her up," the minister said. "I meant the land. There are some gullies that might provide shelter for a man. And a few clusters of trees. That's where he'd head if he was in trouble or just lost his way."

"I could still go with you." Rene sounded tired and not as insistent as she had a minute earlier.

"I know Mandy could use a friend with her," Clay said softly. "I'll be fine with this Conrad fellow."

"And Conrad does know the area." Rene gave a small frown.

"One of the men who prayed for you earlier, Elmer, is getting ready to go, too," the minister said. "That's if there's room in the truck. He wouldn't be able to do much walking in the snow because he has bad knees, but he could be your base person. You'll want someone in the truck to tend the ropes. The other man, Charlie, wanted to go, too, but we decided he should stay here since he's our vet."

"Why would—" Clay started and then he understood.

"He's the closest thing we have to a doctor," the minister finished. "In case the woman goes into labor."

"Then it's good he's staying back." Clay nodded. He wondered if those men were going to insist on praying over him again. If they were, he hoped they waited for him to drink some coffee first. Rene had just turned into the kitchen and he suspected she was going to fix him a cup.

Rene stood at the counter by the sink and frowned at the coffeemaker. The thing wasn't going as fast as it should. Not if she expected to have the thermos filled with hot beverage by the time Clay was ready to leave again. She checked all of the plugs and it should have been working. Maybe if she looked away for a minute, the thing would start to drip.

She was trying to be reasonable. She didn't like being left behind on the final search trip. She had to admit that it made sense to take people who were more familiar with the area, but she worried that something would go wrong. All of the talk about ropes reminded her that Clay would be out in the night in a blizzard with nothing to show him the way back to the truck except for a twisted line of hemp.

What if the old man, Elmer, fell asleep? Or the younger man, Conrad, didn't really know where things were in all of that darkness? Was there a chance Clay could be lost himself?

She heard the coffeemaker signal that the pot was full. She was glad she could at least do this much for him.

Chapter Six

The blizzard had almost completely died down and Rene could see thin streams of light coming through the windows in the pastor's study. Time had slowed down until every second had an impact. She had just finished feeding Mandy some soup and the young woman was calm for the moment.

"Is that them?" Mandy asked as she looked up from the sofa.

She had asked the same question every time there was a door opened or shut in the past hour. But Rene didn't mind.

"Let me go check."

"Wait!" Mandy said before Rene could stand. "How does my hair look? I don't want Davy to see me with funny hair."

"If he knows what's good for him, he'll be glad to see you no matter how your hair looks," Rene said a little fiercely. The more the young woman talked the less Rene was sure that this Davy was good enough for her.

Mandy's voice got quiet. "Do you think he is really going to marry me? My mother used to say he was just taking me for granted."

Rene patted the young woman's hand. What could she say? "If he really is taking you for granted, you're better off without him."

When she met this young man, Rene intended to take him aside and talk to him. He had some explaining to do.

"I wish he'd be a little jealous or something," Mandy continued. She sounded like she wasn't hearing anything Rene was saying. "Just so I'd know he felt the same way I do."

Rene gave up. Pure wistfulness filled Mandy's voice. Being in love could be lonely. Rene knew that. For herself, she was surely missing — Rene stopped. She almost forgot. She should be missing Trace. But the face she wanted to see right now wasn't his. She had a sinking feeling when she realized the face she was hoping to see belonged to Clay. She was no better than Mandy, longing for something that just wasn't there.

"How's she holding up?" Charlie asked as he walked into the room. He'd gone to make another phone call to the small hospital in Miles City.

"Worried," Rene said with a smile toward Mandy.

"They'll be back soon," Charlie said as he bent over Mandy. "Then we'll take you to the hospital. Just as a precaution."

"I could go without Davy if I have to," Mandy said with a quick glance at Rene. "He can follow me for once."

"Good for you," the older man said as he straightened up and looked at Rene. "You need to eat something, too. There's more soup in the kitchen. Go get yourself a bowl. I'll wait with Mandy."

"I'm fine," Rene said.

"That's an order," the older man said. "I don't want to have two patients."

Rene had to admit her legs were a little cramped from sitting on that folding chair. "I'll be back."

"Maybe you can see them from one of the windows," Mandy said.

"I'll look," Rene said as she walked out of the room.

She hadn't let herself think about what it meant that the men weren't back yet. They obviously hadn't found Davy right away or they would all be sitting in the church by now warming up.

Rene walked down the hall and crossed the back of the sanctuary to get to the entryway. She opened the door and walked out on the front steps. The blizzard had stopped and everything was quiet. The sky was growing lighter in the east as the sun started to rise. She looked down the only street and saw the tracks of Clay's truck. The houses were all white with snow, and the little town looked peaceful. There was no sign in the distance of Clay's truck coming home, though.

If there was anything but snow-covered hills around, she would wonder if Davy had taken this opportunity to leave Mandy. It was hard to respect him when he hadn't already married the young woman. No one needed to wait until Idaho to take their wedding vows. Mandy had assured her that they were both eighteen. There were churches all along the road there and any number of ministers willing to marry them. She wondered if the guy was a complete flake.

Rene turned around and went back into the church. All they could do was to wait.

Clay was fed up with love. He and Conrad had managed to find the missing Davy just before daybreak and they'd worked hard to bring him back to the road. The skinny kid had cramps in his legs and his feet were half-frozen. But instead of letting them put him in the truck, he'd used what little strength he had to walk over to the car he'd almost driven in the ditch just hours before. He stood there and refused to go anywhere until Mandy came back.

"I can't leave her. I love her," the exhausted young man said as he held onto the door handle of the car for support.

"She's safe," Conrad told him for the third time, trying to coax him over to the truck. "She's waiting for you in the church in Dry Creek."

Davy looked pathetic, but he didn't move. "She's going to have my baby. She's everything to me. And I haven't even married her."

Clay shook his head. Davy didn't look any older than Mandy. Both of them were too young to be parents, in his opinion. He would have thought the realities of life would have knocked some of that love out of them by now, too. They both talked about it like they were sincere, though.

"Just get in the truck. I'm cold and hungry and your girlfriend is waiting for you at the church—well, unless they found a way to get her to the hospital," Clay said.

"The hospital?" Davy looked up in alarm.

At least that seemed to get the guy's attention. Clay had to admit the young man was probably making all the connections as fast as he could. His brain must be still frozen. Davy had been lost in the snow for hours by the time they found him. Fortunately, he had been wearing a heavy coat and had found a bit of shelter next to some squat trees on the side of a gully.

Davy let go of the door handle to the car and held his hands out to Clay and Conrad. "Take me to her."

"Finally," Clay said as he stepped forward.

By the time they got to the outskirts of town, Davy

seemed reasonably thawed. He was sprawled out between Clay and Elmer on the front seat of the truck. Conrad was squeezed into the small back seat, his legs almost to his chin. No one had the energy to talk or move until Clay drove into town. He wondered if anyone else had managed to get through the snow by now. The blizzard was over and the sun was starting to rise. It made him feel downright triumphant.

Clay honked the horn on his truck briefly. That should get them a welcome.

Sure enough, the door to the church flew open. There had to be a half-dozen people crowded in the doorway. Clay had to squint to figure out which one was Rene.

Elmer opened the passenger side of the truck and climbed down. Clay had his hand on his own door handle when the minister came running up to his window.

"Thank God you're back," the minister said when Clay rolled down his window. "You need to take Mandy to the hospital in Miles City. Something is going wrong."

Clay didn't like the way the minister looked; the man was worried.

"I'm ready to go," Clay said as Conrad climbed out of the backseat and stood by the passenger-side door.

It didn't take more than a few minutes for Rene to squeeze into the backseat and for the men to lift Mandy into the front seat next to Davy.

"Charlie's inside talking to the hospital on the phone," the minister said. "They'll be expecting Mandy. Go now. Call us when you get there."

"Shouldn't Charlie be coming, too?" Clay asked as he looked up at the door of the church. No one else was standing in the opening.

"He gave me instructions," Rene said. "I'm all set."

Clay nodded and the passenger door was closed. Mandy sighed deeply as she leaned against her boyfriend while he put his arm around her. Clay started the truck and backed up so he could turn around to take the road into Miles City.

"Remember to stay calm," Rene said as she reached over and touched Mandy on the shoulder. "Try to think of something else."

"The sun's up," Mandy said. "That's nice."

"Yes, it is," Rene agreed.

Mandy took a quick breath and then closed her eyes on a pain.

"Maybe you should count," Rene said. "Charlie said you needed distractions."

"Charlie's a good man," Clay offered. "It's best to do what he says."

Mandy opened her eyes and looked over at Clay. Rene could see how the sun shined from the east and highlighted Clay's profile. She wasn't sure what Mandy's slight smile meant, though, until the younger woman spoke. "We should add hats to the list."

"Huh?" Davy said as he shifted his arm so it would go behind Mandy more fully. "You want to buy some things? We could do that."

Mandy shook her head. "No, I'm adding it to the husband list. Me and Rene are making our lists."

Rene half-choked. Did Mandy mean she was making a list, too? "I thought you—" Rene stopped. What was Mandy doing?

"A hat just looks so masculine," Mandy continued. "Yes, we definitely want a man with a hat—a big cowboy hat."

"But I wear a cap," Davy protested. "Remember, I like the baseball brim?"

Rene thought she heard Mandy purr for a second and then the younger woman said, "Clay wears a cowboy hat."

Clay could feel everyone in the truck staring at him, and not all of the gazes were friendly. He swore he didn't understand women. He did recognize the glare he was getting from Davy, though. "I hear baseball caps are popular these days."

The young man grunted.

"Not every man can wear a cowboy hat," Rene agreed emphatically.

Clay remembered that Trace wore a Stetson. Of course, Rene would put that on her husband list.

"It's just that a cowboy hat looks so romantic." Mandy finished her comment with a sigh. "And what woman doesn't like a little romance in her life?"

"I can be romantic," Davy said stiffly.

Clay was starting to feel sorry for the young man. Just then Mandy gave a deep gasp that had Clay hunching forward over the steering wheel again. They were a good ten miles from Miles City. Fortunately, the roads had become better as they got closer. The snowplow must have cleaned some of the snow off last night.

They were quiet for miles. Clay figured Mandy and Rene must have given up on their relaxation goal. How could anyone be totally calm when Mandy was sitting there with her lips pressed tightly together in pain?

Clay didn't know what to do about it, but it looked to him like the young woman was going to have her baby early. He was relieved when he saw a cluster of buildings come into view. It was Miles City.

A large sign led to the hospital, and Clay drove the

truck up to the front entrance. Snow covered the parking lot, but there were enough footprints in it to show that the place was open.

Davy was closest to the passenger door and he carefully moved his arm, which was holding Mandy, so that he could open the door.

"I'll come around," Clay said as he turned the engine off.

"Maybe you should go inside and get a wheelchair," Rene said from the back. "Charlie said they have them right inside the door here."

Clay nodded as he opened his door and climbed down. He hurried around the front of his truck and went inside the building.

"Wheelchair?" Clay demanded of a matronly nurse who was walking by. "We have a pregnant woman outside."

"Charlie's girl?"

"Yeah."

"I'll get some help." The nurse turned to the reception area.

Clay thought he could relax once he got Mandy inside the hospital, but he was wrong.

"You're sure you don't know what insurance she has?" the woman at the reception desk was asking Davy. "She said she'd been seeing a doctor in Minneapolis."

"She was at her parents'. It was their insurance," Davy said, leaning on the shelf by the receptionist window.

"Maybe you could call them up and get the information," Rene suggested. She was sitting on a chair nearby.

"I don't know their number. Besides, they hate me."

Clay was standing beside the window and he hadn't said a word. Those two young people thought it was enough that they loved each other, but they were wrong. It was never all a couple needed. He could see why their parents were concerned.

"Can't you just admit her now and figure out the insurance later?" Clay turned slightly so he could smile at the receptionist. Being cordial was the last thing he wanted to do right now, but he didn't see any other way out of this. A smile often worked.

The woman didn't relax a muscle.

"We have policies," she said. "We need to know the bills will be paid when we admit someone."

"I'll pay," Davy said fiercely. "I've got a job waiting for me."

The receptionist looked down at the form Davy had partially filled out. "I don't see your name here. My understanding is that the young lady is not married."

"We're going to get married. We just haven't had time."

Clay was dead tired and he figured there was no way for this conversation to end that was good for anyone. He didn't blame the hospital for not trusting Davy to pay anything. The kid had holes in his blue jeans and didn't look old enough to have a job unless it was in a fast-food place.

"I don't suppose you have a credit card?" The receptionist looked up at Davy. "Or the title to a car or something for a good-faith deposit."

Davy turned his eyes in Clay's direction.

Clay was silent for a moment.

"You can keep this as your deposit," Clay finally said as he undid his belt and pulled it out of the loops on his jeans. "The buckle is solid silver and those stones in the eyes of the bull are real diamonds. It'd sell for a few thousand to someone who collects rodeo buckles. I don't know what it'd bring if you melted it down."

Clay laid the belt out on the counter.

"This is a bit unusual," the receptionist said as she frowned up at Clay. "And you are? Someone's father?"

Clay almost laughed until he realized he was old enough to be the father of either of those kids. "If you have to put something on that form, put that I'm a friend of the family."

Davy reached over and wrapped his arms around Clay. "I'll pay you back."

"Every penny," Clay agreed as he gritted his teeth. Why did everyone want to hug him these days?

His eyes just naturally went over to where Rene was sitting. It wouldn't hurt her to come over and thank him. Maybe give him a little hug herself. She just sat there watching him, though. He was getting that bug-pinned-to-the-wall feeling again, too. He wondered how he had disappointed her this time.

Chapter Seven

"What?" Clay asked as he walked over to where Rene was sitting. He could tell by the slight frown on her face that something didn't please her.

"It's just too bad, that's all," she said, looking tired.

Clay sat down on the hard plastic bench next to her in the waiting room. Squares of linoleum covered the floor beneath their feet and shiny posters on the walls urged everyone to eat more fruits and vegetables.

"What's too bad?" Clay asked gently when Rene didn't go any further. He noticed that the sun was shining in the big windows on the side of the room facing the parking lot. The snow would be melting before long.

"It's just too bad Davy couldn't have come to Mandy's rescue," Rene said finally. Then she turned to him. "She needs to believe that he loves her. But I wonder—do you think he does?"

Clay put his arm along the plastic ridge at the back of the bench. He wasn't the one to ask about these things. "I think he plans to marry her. Whether that makes any sense for either one of them, I don't know."

"But just getting married isn't enough," Rene protested. She moved so she could sit sideways and look at him directly. "Shouldn't he—"

"Make her eyes sparkle and her head spin?" Clay finished for her, so caught up in watching her blue eyes flash and her cheeks grow pink that he forgot he should be careful with his words.

When he remembered how unpopular his opinions on love were with Rene, he swallowed. He was feeling a little warm. He wondered if the temperature was set right in this room.

"Well, yes," Rene admitted. "A woman needs to have that special feeling in her heart telling her that she's loved. That's how she knows it's true."

Clay looked at her. If Trace could see Rene now, he would come running. What man wouldn't? She was so filled with compassion for some young woman she'd just met that it made her eyes glow. She was beautiful. Absolutely, breath-stoppingly gorgeous.

And Clay wanted her all for himself. He swallowed. This wasn't good. The room that had been too hot was suddenly too cold. He felt like he was wearing a tight necktie, but when he put his hand up all he felt were his chin whiskers. He needed to shave. Then he needed to get his head examined. He had nothing to offer a woman like her.

"Maybe he doesn't know how to go about it," Clay finally said. His tongue was thick and his words were slow. "This love stuff."

"He knew how to get her pregnant," Rene snapped right back. "He should know about the rest."

Okay, Clay told himself. He took a breath.

"Some men just aren't much good at talking about their

emotions," Clay managed to say. "Maybe they don't know the words to tell a woman how they feel about her even when they do—you know—feel those things. A lot."

Rene was silent for so long that he thought she must know he was talking about himself. He resisted the urge to pull his hat farther down on his face to hide his eyes. He didn't want to make anyone feel awkward here.

Finally Rene shook her head and said, "No, I think Davy is just scared."

"Well, he should be scared." Clay told himself he was relieved Rene hadn't read anything into his words. It was for the best. It had been a crazy impulsive hope on his part anyway. "The poor kid's clueless about being a husband and a father. I don't think he's even old enough to vote."

Clay wondered if the reason his emotions were flipping around like this was because he hadn't eaten anything since yesterday. That must be it. Or maybe it was because he hadn't slept in over twenty-four hours and this room was too warm.

"It's not that bad," Rene said with a smile. "Mandy told me they both turned eighteen last winter."

Clay looked around. There had to be a vending machine somewhere. The place didn't look big enough to have a caféteria, but he'd settle for a candy bar. After he ate something, he'd rest his eyes. Until then, he focused on Rene. He was getting his footing back.

"Maybe Davy doesn't want to make her feel like she's loved until he can take care of her," Clay told Rene. "There's more to love than just the way someone feels. A man has a lot of responsibilities."

"And you think a young mother doesn't?"

Clay really needed to find a vending machine. He was getting a headache.

"I think a young mother is a pillar of civilization. Her job is more important than anyone's," he said. He thought he saw a large silver machine at the end of the hall to his right. "Could I get you a candy bar?"

"I don't have any change."

"It's my treat," he said.

"Oh, I couldn't—"

Clay stood up. He didn't have all day. "I'll put it on your tab."

Rene smiled. "Well, then, maybe something with nuts in it."

Clay nodded. They'd both feel better if they had something to eat.

Rene listened to Clay's footsteps as he walked down the hall. She liked just listening to his strong, confident steps on the linoleum. She'd never noticed the sound a man made with his boots before.

She shook her head. If she gave any weight to her feelings right now, she'd be making a mistake. Lately, when Clay tipped back his hat so he could look at her long and steady, she found her heart pounding a little faster and her hands trembling. Those, not to mention the footstep issue, were classic signs of true smitten love. He could twirl his finger and she'd be enthralled. That's how it happened.

But Clay didn't see her as anything more than a customer. Her problem with Trace had been that she had let her feelings guide her instead of waiting for other signs of love. She wasn't going to make the same mistake with Clay. She was going to finish that list of what she needed in a husband and she was going to abide by it.

Still, when Clay walked back into the waiting room, her

heart felt a little happier at the sight of him. He'd taken off his coat and he was wearing one of those cowboy shirts with all of the snaps. She'd never noticed how really fine those shirts looked on a man, especially when he had on well-worn jeans and leather cowboy boots. She didn't suppose she could add "must wear boots" to her list.

"I got you a caramel nut thing," Clay said as he sat back down next to her and held out the wrapped candy bar. "I looked for some coffee, too, but they didn't have any."

Rene nodded as she took the candy. "They probably figure worry keeps people awake in a place like this."

Clay nodded as he took the wrapping off the plain chocolate bar he held. "I stopped and asked the receptionist. She said things were going okay with Mandy, but we wouldn't hear anything for a while."

"Well, I suppose that's good news," Rene said.

Clay nodded. "She said we should try to get some sleep."

"I don't think anyone could sleep on these things." Rene took a bite of her candy bar as she shifted on the hard plastic bench beneath her.

"Well, I aim to find out," Clay said.

Rene barely finished her candy bar before her eyes started to feel tired. She told herself it would do her good to close them for a few minutes. Maybe it'd even get her emotions back on an even level. Clay had pulled his hat down past his eyes and was leaning back on the bench. He'd been so quiet she thought he might actually be dozing. She would just put her head back and relax a little, too.

The sun woke Rene much later. At first, she thought she was home in her bed in Mule Hollow. But her pillow was firm and her neck was at an odd angle. Then her eyes flew open and she sat up straight.

"I'm sorry, I—" Rene stammered. She'd been leaning against Clay's shoulder while she was sleeping.

"No problem. I thought it was kind of nice," Clay said with his slow smile. His hat was sitting beside him on the bench and his dark hair was tousled. She could see where she'd wrinkled his shirt a little by laying against it.

"Yes, well, I—" Rene stopped herself. What could she say? "These benches really are not made for sleeping."

"I don't know." Clay's eyes were filled with warmth. "I slept fine."

If she didn't know better, Rene would have said Clay was flirting with her. Well, maybe not flirting, but beaming at her with affection in his eyes. She'd blame it on poor lighting, but sunshine was streaming in through the window.

"They haven't told us any more about Mandy, have they?" Rene said. She needed to remember why they were here. Maybe Clay had just heard some good news and that's why he was so happy.

Clay shook his head.

"Well, at least there's no bad news. They'd tell us if something was wrong," Rene said as she stood up. "I think I'll go ask the nurse how things are going."

"They won't tell you much," Clay said. "Patient confidentiality."

"Yeah, well, I'll ask anyway."

Clay watched Rene run away. She was embarrassed, and she didn't even know the half of it. She had snuggled against his arm when she was asleep like she was born to it. He'd never had a sweeter moment's rest than with her lying against his shoulder.

Sometime while she slept, he had realized he was at a crossroads. He wasn't sure he could keep to the same path he'd always walked. Uncle Prudy had warned him that he might want to have a fuller life someday. He hadn't believed him, but here it was. He was like the proverbial kid with his nose pressed against a store window and nothing in his pocket to buy what he desired with all of his heart.

The truth was, Clay realized, that he had no idea how to make this new life he wanted. He was used to motel rooms and solitary meals. What did he know about being part of a family? But having Rene pressed so close to him for these past few hours made him want to try.

Just then he saw a flash of movement out the window. The sun had continued to shine all morning. Puddles were forming and snow was dripping off the cars in the parking lot.

Clay stood up to look closer and saw the minister out there helping his wife walk to the hospital entrance. They both wore long coats and Rene's aunt was using her crutches. Clay was worried she might slip until he noticed that her husband was walking just enough ahead of her so he could catch her if she did.

Those were two people who knew what it meant to love each other, Clay thought. He had known that from seeing them earlier that night. No wonder Rene had fallen for Trace so easily. Her whole family seemed to accept love as the natural way to live.

His life had taught him the opposite. He could still remember his mother's bitter complaints about her life and husband, even after the man was dead. Clay wondered what kind of a person his father had been, but all he knew is that the man treasured a gold tie tack shaped like a cross. That did not tell Clay much. He needed more. He had no more of an idea about how to be a husband and father than young Davy did.

But that minister outside the window knew all about it.

Clay stood watching Rene's aunt and uncle until they reached the cement pad outside the hospital entrance. Then he walked out of the waiting room so he could greet them.

Rene looked up from the receptionist's desk when the door opened to the hospital. Rene smiled when she saw her aunt step through the door, followed by her uncle.

"How did you get here?" Rene asked as she walked over to hug them. "I thought everything was still blocked."

"The snowplow cleared the roads to Dry Creek," her aunt said as she reached out her arm to Rene. "And we wanted to know how Mandy is doing."

Rene turned back to look at the receptionist. "She said things are going well. And Davy is going to come out and see us in a minute."

"There's room in here to sit, Mrs. Curtis," Clay said as he walked out of the waiting room and looked at Rene's aunt. "We need to be sure the snow is all off the bottom of your cane, too. You can lean on me if you need."

"Why, that would be lovely. But call me Glory. Aunt Glory, if you want."

Clay nodded.

Rene wanted to crawl under one of those cold hard benches in the other room. She needed to talk to her aunt. In private. Rene knew her family was filled with hopeless romantics, but it was embarrassing to have her aunt assume Clay even wanted to be that close to them. He had made his position on romantic love pretty clear on the drive up here.

"Maybe you could come with me to get a can of soda," Rene said to her aunt. "The machine's just down the hall."

"I could—" her uncle started to offer.

Rene's aunt shook her head and turned to her husband. "I'll go. It'll give you a chance to have a nice chat with Clay."

With that, the two women started down the hallway.

Clay had a bad feeling. The couple had obviously discussed having a chat with him, and the minister had been assigned the task. Well, he supposed he couldn't blame them. It wouldn't have taken them long to figure out that he wasn't good enough for their niece. They probably thought they were doing him a kindness to warn him off. Although that didn't make any sense, with her aunt inviting him to call her by her first name. Of course, that could be guilt. Some people were like that.

Clay squared his shoulders. He knew how to take his falls.

"How's your cold?" Clay asked as he turned to lead into the waiting room.

"Better. Thanks," the minister said as he followed Clay.

Both men sat down on the hard benches.

The minister turned to Clay. "I've been wanting to talk to you."

Clay nodded. "I have the highest respect for your niece."

"Oh," the minister said as he looked at Clay in slight surprise.

"Of course, nothing happened between us on the road up here," Clay added. If he didn't know better, he thought he might be blushing. He never blushed. Not that anyone could see it through all of the whiskers on his face if he did.

"Really," the minister said with even more interest.

Clay didn't know how much more of this he could take. "So, you see, there's no need for us to have a talk."

"Really," the minister repeated, only this time he was grinning. "Rene's aunt and I wanted to offer to pay her towing bill. I wanted to know how much it is."

"I see," Clay said. He'd done it this time. "That's very nice of you."

"Rene means a lot to us," the minister said. His smile slowed down some, but not much. "She's an easy woman to love."

Clay looked at the floor. He could see where they had tracked mud and snow in. It needed a good washing. He could look at the floor all day, but he had never been a coward, so he lifted his eyes again.

"I'm not good enough for her," he said to the minister. "I want to be, but I don't know how."

The smile on the minister's face slowed down until it became a look of compassion. "I've noticed the cross you wear. Tell me about it."

"It's an old tie tack. Belonged to my father. I never knew him, but he left it to me when he died. My mother didn't think much of it. Said it was a poor man who didn't have anything else to give to his only son."

The minister put a hand on Clay's shoulder. "I'm not so sure I agree with her. It seems like a fine legacy."

Just then the two women walked back into the room.

"We'll talk later," the minister said to Clay as he stood up to help his wife sit down.

"I saw Davy coming down the hall," Rene said as she kept standing. "He's got news and he's coming this way."

Chapter Eight

"It's okay," Davy said as he walked into the waiting room. "They've stopped the contractions. Mandy has to keep still for the next month, but the baby's okay and she's okay and it's all just okay."

Davy collapsed onto the bench closest to him. "I never want to go through this again."

Rene didn't have the heart to tell him that the actual birth of his child wasn't going to be any easier. The poor boy looked exhausted.

"Can Mandy have visitors?" Rene asked.

"They're getting her ready to go home," Davy said.

There was silence in the room.

Finally Clay spoke. "Your car's stuck in a snowdrift. I guess I could go dig it out for you."

Davy sat straight up. "I forgot. We don't have any place to go." His eyes grew panicked. "Where will I take her? She's supposed to be lying down for the next month."

Rene's aunt and uncle exchanged a glance. Rene knew what they were thinking.

"We've got an extra bedroom. You can bring her to our place until we find somewhere for you to stay until the baby's born," her uncle said as he leaned forward toward Davy. "Now's not the time to worry. You need to stay calm for Mandy. We have twin boys that can be a little loud, but they're visiting their grandmother in Havre right now."

Davy slumped in relief. "I'll make it up to you. Odd jobs. Anything."

"We'll talk about that later." Rene's uncle said.

Rene was proud of him. Mandy and Davy would be in good hands while they waited for their baby. Just then a nurse wheeled Mandy into the room.

"Well, hello," Rene said as she stood up and walked to the young woman before bending down to give her a hug. Mandy's face was pale, but she didn't look like she was in any pain.

Davy was there, too, whispering in her ear, "We're going to stay in Dry Creek for a while. With these kind people."

Mandy gave a long relieved sigh and then sat up straighter and looked at her boyfriend. "But what about your job in Idaho?"

"I'll call them," Davy said. "The most important thing is the baby."

"You won't go ahead without me, will you?" Mandy's eyes were anxious.

Rene drew in a gasp. Mandy shouldn't even have to ask that question. Rene was going to say something, but she felt a comforting hand on her back. She stood up and Clay was there.

"I'm not going anywhere without you," Davy declared emphatically. He stood tall when he said it, too, like he was making a pledge.

Rene was glad Clay had stopped her from spoiling this moment. Mandy's eyes were flowing over with tears and her face was beaming.

The nurse standing behind Mandy cleared her voice. "Someone needs to bring their car up to the front so we can put Mandy inside."

"Our car is probably the easiest for her to get into," Rene's uncle said. "I'll go get it."

Clay nodded. "There's nothing easy about climbing into a truck."

The nurse turned to wheel Mandy toward the door and everyone else followed.

Rene and Clay were walking past the receptionist's desk when the woman called out to them.

"Don't forget—" the receptionist said as she held up Clay's belt.

Clay turned back. "I thought you needed it for your payment."

The receptionist nodded to Mandy and Davy as they went out of the hospital. "She had the phone number for her parents in her purse and he called them to get her insurance information. So, it's all squared away."

"Well, then," Clay said as he took the belt. "Thanks."

Rene watched as Clay looped his belt around his jeans. "That was nice of you, putting your buckle up as payment when they needed it."

"It's only silver," Clay said as they walked to the door. He looked down at her. "Well, there's the diamonds, too."

Rene didn't know many men who would be so casual about a hunk of metal, especially when it was an award for something they had done.

When she stepped outside, Rene looked at her uncle's

car. It was full with Davy and Mandy in the backseat and her aunt's crutches leaning against the inside of the passenger-side door.

"We'll follow you to make sure you don't have any trouble," Clay said as they walked past the car. She had no choice but to go with him, but it made her feel good, like they were a couple.

Besides, not only was Clay generous with his silver, he was thoughtful, too.

"Our house is the big white one right next to the church," Rene's uncle said. "We'll see you there."

Rene told herself it was time to stop thinking about Clay.

Clay walked beside Rene on the way to his truck. He remembered how Rene's uncle had walked with his wife and wondered if he should do the same with Rene. He had a suspicion he would irritate her if it was too obvious that he was worried she might slip on the slush and mud.

Trying to think like a husband would take some getting used to.

"Do you have a lot of those belts?" Rene asked suddenly. "The ones with those championship buckles?"

Clay nodded as they arrived at his truck. "I have my share."

He started to walk around the truck to his door when he saw Rene's frown. He had forgotten to open her door.

"Sorry about that," Clay muttered as he stepped up to the passenger door and opened it.

Rene's frown didn't go away. "So do they have groupies in the rodeo? Like rock stars do?"

Clay looked down at her in bewilderment. "You mean like women screaming and fainting?"

Rene looked up at him and nodded.

"Well, I guess people put a bit of effort into applauding the winners," Clay admitted. He didn't think Rene was asking about the women who wanted to take a rodeo champion home with them for the night.

"Well, you could have told me," Rene said as she climbed up into his truck. "I wouldn't have bored you with my broken heart if I had known you had women throwing themselves at you all day long."

Clay stood there speechless. Okay, so maybe the nighttime thing *had* been what she'd been asking. Did that mean she cared?

"We better get going," Rene finally said. "My uncle's just pulling out of the parking lot."

Clay had no choice but to walk around to the driver's door and climb into the truck himself. He turned the ignition on, but decided to wait on the heater. The sun was warming the truck up nicely.

"I didn't have women throwing themselves at me," Clay said as he drove up behind the car. Rene's uncle pulled out on the main road. "Not like in those rock star concerts. No one ever tried to climb up into the chute with me or anything."

"That's all right," Rene said. "It's none of my business."

Clay was tempted to tell her just how much of her business it was, but he didn't want to confess how he felt about her when she was annoyed with him. There was no sense in giving her any more excuses than she already had to shut him down.

The mud on the roads made driving almost as difficult as the snow did. Clay kept a close eye on the car ahead of him as it made another turn to follow the road to Dry Creek.

"Nice day out there," Clay offered by way of conversation when they'd gone a half mile or so.

"It's still too wet to start on that mural," Rene said. She was slumped against the passenger door again, looking discouraged. "We can't paint when it's like this."

"It'll dry out soon," Clay said and then realized he should add a little more if he wanted to do his share of the talking on the way back. Rene liked to have someone to talk to her. "You never did tell me about the mural."

Rene looked up. "It's going to be a historical picture."

"Really?"

Rene nodded, shifting on the seat so she could look at him. "My aunt says that years ago there was a community barn rising just outside of Dry Creek. The barn's still there. She wants to paint a scene of that happening on the side of the place. We'll show faces and figures, all working on the barn. She doesn't have many pictures so we're going to make most of it up."

"You'll do great at that," Clay said. That didn't sound like enough, so he added, "With your creativity."

He hadn't known talking to a woman could be so hard. Rene smiled and he relaxed.

"Maybe Mandy can help," Rene said. "I could draw sketches of the figures my aunt is planning for the mural and Mandy could critique them from her bed. My aunt has some old costume books and Mandy can use them to check to see we have things right. It'll give her something to do until the baby comes."

"That'll be something. Seeing the two of them as parents." It hit Clay like a newsflash that the baby was coming in a month and he would be gone in a day or two. He wouldn't see the couple and their baby. His job was done. He had no excuse to stay; he couldn't expect his uncle to cover his business forever, and this town was Rene's refuge, not his.

It was silent.

"You'll have to send me a picture of them," Clay finally said. He was miserable.

Rene couldn't think of anything to say, so she nodded. She wasn't ready for Clay to leave. She could hardly ask him to stay, though. He'd already done her a huge service just by bringing her here. "If you wait a bit, I can earn enough to write you a check."

"I trust you for it. You can mail it," Clay said. "Or, maybe, you could keep the check and bring it to Mule Hollow when you come to see your cousin."

"Yes, I could do that," Rene said with pleasure. At least she'd have a reason to see Clay in the future.

"I forgot about Trace," Clay said with an indrawn breath. "Coming to Mule Hollow might be difficult."

"Oh," Rene said with a pause. She couldn't just declare herself over Trace without looking a little unstable. "Maybe he will be out of town or something when I come."

There was no way Rene was going to give up a chance to see Clay again. They were both silent until they arrived at the house where her aunt and uncle lived.

Chapter Nine

Clay was sitting in the cab working the levers to lower Davy's car off the back of his tow truck. A full twenty-four hours had passed since Mandy and Davy had come back from the hospital and moved into the downstairs bedroom at the house. Everyone—well, mostly Rene—had been busy getting the young couple settled in. If Clay didn't know better, he would think Rene was avoiding him.

Maybe she just thought he had his chores, too. First, he had unloaded her car from the back of his tow truck so he could go pick up Davy's car. Rene seemed to appreciate that he had done both of those things. He wasn't sure why she didn't look him in the eye anymore.

It could be the money, he thought to himself as he watched Davy's car touch the ground. He should tell her he didn't care about her towing bill. Her aunt and uncle had not said anything more to him about paying it, but he was fine if it never got paid. His uncle had been right. Even with the hours they'd spent worrying in the hospital, this trip had been better than any vacation he'd ever taken. It was because Rene had been with him.

Clay got the car to the ground and stepped outside to finish unhooking it. Then he heard the sound of footsteps behind him and he turned.

"Got a minute?" Rene's uncle asked as he walked closer. The man had clearly been at the church and was walking back to his house.

"Sure."

"I've been looking for something I wanted to give you all morning," the minister said as he held out a small book. "I knew I had it and I finally found it."

Clay took the black book in his hand and turned it over so he could see the front of it.

"It's called *The Cross Explained*," the minister said. "I thought you might want to read it since you have your father's tie tack. Maybe it'll tell you why that cross was so important to him."

"It's mighty slim to say all that," Clay said as he eyed the book.

"There's nothing too complicated about the cross of the Bible," the minister said with a smile. "It's all about Our Father's love for His children. The sacrifice He made for us. The new chances He offers."

Clay snorted softly at that. "Now that's what I could use. A chance to be a new kind of man."

The minister nodded. "Then you need to meet God. Why don't we go someplace and sit down to talk?"

Clay hesitated and then decided he had nothing to lose. "Sure."

Clay didn't see the curtain move as he walked toward the church.

Rene pulled away from the window. She had been watching Clay all morning. Not constantly, of course, but here and there, between doing things like folding towels at the dining room table for her aunt, she had looked out the window just to reassure herself that Clay was still there. Now, she saw that Clay was going over to the church with her uncle and it made her sigh.

"Anything interesting out the window?" her aunt asked from where she leaned against the doorjamb into the kitchen.

"Uh, no, not really," Rene said as she turned and walked back to the table with the towels on it. "Just Clay unloading Davy's car."

Her aunt limped over to one of the dining room chairs and sat down. "I thought it might be him. He's an interesting young man."

Rene picked up a towel and started to fold it. "He can be exasperating."

"I imagine so," her aunt agreed calmly.

Rene finished with the towel and reached for another before she drew in her breath and began. "I think I'm adopted."

"Good gracious, why do you say that?" her aunt asked in astonishment. "I was at the hospital when you were born."

"Then how come I can't recognize true love?"

"Are you feeling some special love for someone?" her aunt asked with a smile.

"I don't know." Rene sighed. "But I do know I was wrong when I thought Trace and I were falling in love. And everyone in the family has known who they loved almost at first sight. And there's Grandma's veil and—I'm a failure at it all."

"Whoa," her aunt said with a small frown. "Who said everyone in the family falls in love at first sight?"

"Well, don't they? You did. My mother—"

"Your mother fell in love at first sight almost eight months after she met your father. She couldn't stand him at first. Thought he was too arrogant."

"Really?" Rene frowned. Her mother had never told her that.

"After your dad died, your mom just liked to remember it a little bit differently."

"Really?" Rene let it all sink in. "I still don't know, though. It doesn't work so well for me. I think I'd be better off making a list. Especially if—" Rene stopped. "Oh, well, I might as well say it, especially if Clay's the one. He's not into emotions very much, and I think he'd like a list."

"Well, whatever you do, I know you'll want to pray about it."

Rene froze. She tried to stop the dismay from covering her face. "Maybe you could pray for me."

Her aunt was silent for a few minutes.

"Rene, what's wrong?"

"Nothing. I just—that is—God and I—we just—" Rene looked at her aunt's face. She didn't see anything but love, and she had kept everything inside for so long. "God doesn't like me anymore."

Her aunt got up from her chair and limped over to where Rene sat. Then she bent down and hugged her close. "Why do you say that, dear?"

"I don't feel Him with me anymore. Not since mom died," Rene whispered. "I was mad at Him and now He's mad at me."

"Oh, my dear, God understands why you were angry. It's okay. He still loves you. He never stopped caring for you. He's always with you."

Rene started to cry in her aunt's arms.

"Here." After a few minutes, her aunt offered her one of the fresh towels lying on the table. "He always provides for our needs, too. Even if its just terrycloth when we need it."

Rene smiled at that as she wiped her eyes with the hand towel.

"Now," her aunt said as she stood up and limped back to her original chair, "what's on this list you're making? I've always thought a husband should be handy around the house."

"Clay doesn't know much about houses," Rene said.

Her aunt nodded. "Then put down that he should be good with horses."

Rene giggled. "I can't make a list just for him."

"Why not?" her aunt asked with a wave of her hand. "That's what your mother would do. We'll start a new family tradition."

Clay never thought he would know what his father was like. But he did. He had been a man of faith. What more did a son need to know to follow in his footsteps? The minister had only been talking for a few minutes when Clay felt deeply that his life had been leading to this moment. He wondered if his father had prayed for him before he died. Prayed that this moment would come, when Clay would meet God and know why his father had cherished that small cross.

The emotions stirred so deeply inside him that he was scared. He didn't trust himself. He wasn't supposed to have feelings like that. To his surprise, though, the minister accepted it all like it was natural.

Clay spent an hour with the minister before he needed to come up for air.

"We can continue later," Rene's uncle finally said and then hesitated. "My wife and I are hoping you can stay for a while."

"I don't want to put you out." Clay had already talked with Uncle Prudy and found out that there had only been three calls for a tow job in his absence. His uncle could handle that kind of volume easily.

"I've made some phone calls. I hope you don't mind. But if you want some work, Conrad's garage in Miles City has some jobs you could do. And I need help putting up scaffolding for the women before they start that mural."

"They're going to use scaffolding?" Clay asked in alarm. "When Rene said they were painting a barn, I thought she meant a short barn. Something close to the ground. Maybe a shed even."

Rene's uncle shook his head. "The thing has to be almost thirty feet up there."

"And you're letting your wife do that?" Clay demanded.

The minister chuckled. "I can see you'll have some surprises in store for you when you get married."

"Oh," Clay let the man's words settle in to his heart. For the first time, it seemed possible.

"Well?"

Clay nodded. "If you're building scaffolding, I'm going to be there to help and to make sure the bracing is strong."

"Good."

"I can't keep sleeping in your sons' room, though," Clay said. "Aren't they coming back in a couple of days?"

"There's a room for rent down the street I could line up for you. It wouldn't cost much. It's just a room with a bath over a garage."

"I'll take it," Clay said with a grin.

"Well, let's get to it then," the minister said with a satisfied look on his face.

Clay started over to the house to get his duffle bag. He'd just as soon put it in his room so everyone would know he was staying in Dry Creek. And, if he felt like whistling as he walked back and forth, he saw no reason to hold back.

Rene moved when she saw Clay walking toward the house. She should be pairing up socks at the table and working on her list. So she quickly sat down so Clay wouldn't know she'd been watching for him at the window. Then she put a few socks on top of her list so he wouldn't know she was doing that, either.

"Good afternoon," Clay said when he opened the door and saw Rene.

"I didn't know you whistled," Rene said. "What's new?"

Clay stopped and grinned at her. "Me."

"That's nice," Rene said as she looked at him. He did seem different. "You're not wearing your hat! I can see your eyes."

"Oh." Clay stopped. "I guess I forgot it over in the church."

Rene kept looking at him. He was more relaxed than she could remember seeing him. Of course, he wasn't driving in a snowstorm and he'd been getting enough sleep. She probably looked more peaceful, too.

"Hey, you're working on your list," Clay said as he looked at the table.

Rene turned. Sure enough, the paper showed through the socks.

"You need to put that he has to be a man of faith," Clay said. "On your list. That's what you need."

Rene winced. That would eliminate Clay right then and there. And he sounded pretty cheerful about that fact.

"I have some serious items on the list," Rene said just to show him that he didn't need to worry she was targeting him. "I might even put down a college degree."

"Humm," Clay said, but he wasn't paying any attention. He was looking around the room. "You didn't see what happened to my duffle bag, did you? I thought it was in the corner over there and—"

"It's on the kitchen porch," Rene said. "We didn't want anyone to trip over it."

"Thanks," Clay said as he started walking in that direction. "I'll have it out of your hair in a minute."

Rene stopped cold. He was leaving. She didn't want him to go.

"We're having chicken pot pie for supper," Rene said. "My aunt's recipe."

"Sounds good," Clay said he stepped back into the dining room with his duffle bag in one hand. "I'll be back in time. I'm just going to move into my new place."

"What?"

"A room down the street." Clay was walking through the living room and he turned back when he got to the screen door. "I'm renting it for a couple of weeks."

"Oh," Rene said. When Clay had turned, the afternoon sun was shining in through the open door. He had a golden look to him. He grinned at her and then he stepped through the door.

Rene could hear him whistling as he walked down the street. She still didn't know what he had to be so happy about.

Chapter Ten

Clay was putting on a navy tie. He didn't own a tie, but the minister had been kind enough to lend him one. Clay had been in Dry Creek a week already, and he was driving himself crazy wondering when he was going to have the nerve to talk to Rene about that list of hers.

Well, it wasn't just the list. It was his chances in general with her.

It was Saturday night and he'd asked her to dinner at the Dry Creek Café. It was a date and he'd made some special arrangements with the woman who owned the place. He wanted to grab as many points on that list of hers as he could tonight.

Clay knew it was too soon to ask Rene the big question, but he planned to ask some smaller ones just to give himself hope that there would be a time when he could ask her to marry him without leaving her dumbstruck because she'd had no idea it was even a remote possibility.

He didn't like the idea of shocking Rene with his question.

The tie wasn't knotting right. He scowled at himself in

his bathroom mirror. Maybe wearing a suit was a mistake. He'd had to borrow the suit, too, and he hoped Rene didn't recognize it since it, too, belonged to her uncle just like the tie did.

He wanted to show Rene that he was flexible, though. He had a feeling she'd put something on her list about the man being able to wear a suit. He looked at the clock on his wall. He had to hurry or he wouldn't be on time.

Ten minutes later, Clay was standing at the door, ringing the bell.

Rene heard the doorbell ring and she ran her fingers over her hair again. She'd gone through every item of clothing she owned and had finally given up and put on her long black skirt and the white lace blouse her cousin had given her last Christmas. Rene had just decided the combination made her look like she was waiting tables at a five-star restaurant. But it was too late. There was no time to change.

She picked up her purse and headed downstairs. She'd been anxious all day, except when she'd been terrified. This could be it. Clay had told her he was wearing a suit for dinner. Clay in a suit had to be something. She wondered if he was going to tell her he was leaving Dry Creek.

Whichever it was, she hoped he told her quickly and put her out of her misery. She hadn't been able to eat anything all day, and she wasn't sure she could eat tonight. She had her list in her purse for comfort.

"Oh," Rene said when she opened the door. The porch light was on and she didn't even recognize Clay. "You look—good."

Clay smiled. He wasn't wearing a hat and she could see

the warmth in his eyes. His smile curled her toes. "Here. These are for you."

He held out a dozen pink roses. "They'll need water."

Rene nodded. She could use a little water herself. "I'll just—I mean, come in and I'll put them in a vase before we go."

Rene knew there were six other people in the house tonight, but they were all hidden away in their rooms, even her twin cousins.

"You look beautiful," Clay said as they walked into the kitchen.

The lights were off in the kitchen and Rene turned on the small one over the sink. Her aunt kept the vases under the sink, and Rene bent down to get one. When she stood back up, Clay was close.

She wondered if he was going to kiss her. Hope that he would kept her rooted to where she stood. Clay hesitated for a minute, but he didn't lean down and kiss her. Instead, he stepped around her and started the water running in the sink. Then he slipped the vase under the water. "I'll have it all ready for you in a minute."

Rene nodded. "Are the roses so I remember you?"

"Sure. I guess."

Rene almost started to cry. If it was to remember him, that must mean he was going to tell her he was leaving. It made sense. Clay and her uncle had finished building the scaffolding. He'd done a few towing jobs for Conrad's garage, but someone else could do that. He probably thought it was time for him to go home.

Well, if this was their goodbye dinner, she wanted to be sure that he remembered her, too, and not because she'd spent the evening crying.

* * *

Clay opened the door to the café. The lights were dimmed just like he'd requested. And there was one table sitting in the middle of the eating area. Everything else had been pushed to the side.

"You're sure they're open," Rene asked as she followed him inside.

Okay, so maybe he'd overdone the low lighting, but he didn't want Rene to see the table until they were closer.

"It's closed to everyone but us. Here, take my hand."

Rene slipped her smooth hand into his. He wished he'd realized sooner that the darkness would give him an excuse to hold her hand.

"Careful," Clay said. He could see the outline of the center table.

Clay led Rene to the table and pulled out her chair. Then he walked around and sat in his own chair.

"We're seated," Clay said, loud enough to be heard by the people in the kitchen.

Right on cue, the door opened behind Clay and three young women holding tall candles came out singing. Clay had wanted to get a violin player, but the only person available to play an instrument had been a teenager on a trumpet. So Linda, the owner of the café, had suggested the trio from the church choir.

"Oh," Rene said in awe.

Enough candlelight was shining out that Clay could see the delight on Rene's face. And she hadn't even looked down at the table yet.

"They're beautiful," Rene whispered. "Their voices are magnificent."

Clay suspected the trio might sound magnificent partly

because they were humming "Amazing Grace." They hadn't had time to practice a love song for his dinner, so he told them the hymn would do fine.

The three young women brought their candles to a candelabra standing to the side of the table where Clay and Rene sat. When they put the candles in their place, they walked silently back to the kitchen.

"Oh, my," Rene said. She had finally looked down at the table.

Clay had bought more pink roses when he went into Miles City earlier today. He'd put the best of them in the bouquet, but he had the petals from two dozen more strewn around the table.

Clay figured that, between the roses and the candles, he was doing all he could to set the mood for the kind of floaty love Rene was partial to. Her eyes were glistening in delight and he was satisfied.

"Linda said we have our choice of steak or salmon," Clay noted.

Everything was timed just right.

"I'm not sure I could eat a steak," Rene whispered. "Maybe the salmon."

"Two salmons then," Clay said, again loud enough for people to hear in the kitchen.

Clay congratulated himself. Everything was going better than he would have thought. Now if he could just get his piece said.

"There's something I want to tell you," Clay began.

Rene looked at him and he noticed that the shine in her eyes was not excitement; it was tears.

"What's wrong?" he asked softly.

"Noth-thing," she said as a tear rolled down her cheek. "Please go on."

He reached across the table and wiped the tear off her cheek. He didn't know what he had done, but he had obviously made a bad step somewhere.

"I'm sorry," she choked out. Then she took a long, shuddering breath. "I didn't want to cry. I wanted you to remember me smiling."

Clay felt his heart stop. For a moment, he couldn't speak.

"I don't want to remember you smiling," he said. "I want to see you doing it as often as I can."

"But Mule Hollow is too far away for that," Rene wailed.

"I thought you were staying here. At least until your aunt's mural is done."

Rene lifted her head and looked at him. "Aren't you heading back to Mule Hollow?"

Clay shook his head. "Not anytime soon."

"Well then what am I supposed to remember?"

"Apparently me making a fool of myself," Clay said.

Rene stopped crying and just looked at him for a moment. "Maybe I'm a little bit of a fool, too."

Clay had to admit the candlelight had been a good idea. He could always talk to Rene more easily when they were in the shadows. It reminded him of being in the truck with her. "I guess it's what I get for trying to make it onto your husband list."

"What?" Rene said.

"I know you're not taking applications or anything. But that list you're making. I wanted to hit at least a few of the things on it. We have a flaming dessert later, too."

Rene was smiling now. "Let me show you my list."

She reached down and opened her purse, pulling out a piece of paper.

"Here." She handed him her list.

At first, Clay wondered if the dim light was tricking his eyes.

"Horses. He has to be good with horses," Clay said as he looked up from the list. "And cowboy boots. I have those. And kind eyes, I—" He looked across the table at Rene.

She nodded.

Clay looked back down at the list. He met everything on the list.

"I know it's too soon," he said, staring into her eyes, "but when some time has passed, and I finish the studies your uncle has set out for me, I plan to ask you to marry me, Rene Mitchell."

Clay felt a little dizzy. He was looking at Rene and she was smiling at him.

"I feel funny," Clay muttered. "Not bad, just—"

"Floaty?" Rene asked.

He nodded. "And a little like—well, like the rest of the world isn't here."

He stood up thinking it might clear his head. It didn't. Fortunately, Rene stood, too, and walked around the edge of the table to steady him. A good thirty seconds passed before everything became clear for Clay. "I'm falling in love. It's not just love, it's the 'falling into' kind."

"It's the good stuff," Rene ended for him.

Clay grinned down at her. "It sure is."

Then he bent his head to kiss her.

Epilogue

A month and a half later, Rene twirled around in her wedding dress, her great-grandmother's veil flowing with her. Splashes of blue forget-me-knots shone in the mirror in the midst of all the white netting.

"It's time," her cousin, Paisley, announced from the doorway with a wide grin.

Rene had used her uncle's study to change into her clothes for the wedding. She couldn't believe she was really getting married. "I'm coming."

"You're a beautiful bride," Paisley whispered as they walked out of the study.

They both peeked around the corner to the sanctuary and saw the church filled with roses. Pink ones. Red ones. And a few white ones. Clusters of the flowers were tied with ribbons to the pews. Two big bouquets graced the front where Clay stood in his tuxedo and waited for Rene. His Uncle Prudy stood next to him as his best man. And the people of Dry Creek filled the pews with their support and good wishes. Mandy and Davy and their new baby boy sat in the front row.

"You're next," Rene said to her cousin. "Someday soon love will just hit you and it'll all be over except for the wedding ceremony. Just give me a call and I'll send this veil back to Mule Hollow when that happens."

"I won't need it any time soon."

"You'll want more than a teaching career some day," Rene said as she leaned over and kissed her cousin on the cheek.

Just then the organ music started and Paisley began her walk down the aisle as the bridesmaid. Rene took a deep breath and enjoyed the fragrance of the roses. Every time she smelled a rose now she thought of Clay.

It was time. She stepped out to the aisle and saw Clay's face. She hadn't wanted anyone to walk her down the aisle, but she was grateful for Clay's steady gaze pulling her to him.

Clay took her hand when she walked up to him and they turned to her uncle.

The vows went all too quickly. Before she knew it, Paisley had stepped up to pin back her veil.

"I now pronounce you man and wife," Rene heard her uncle say. "You may kiss the bride."

Clay wasn't rushing. Rene watched his eyes as he slowly traced her jaw with his thumb. She trembled as his eyes told her she was precious to him. Only then did he dip his head and kiss her. She felt his love completely.

* * * * *

A MULE HOLLOW MATCH
Debra Clopton

This book is dedicated to Chase, Kris
and Heidi with much love

In my distress I called to the Lord, and he answered me; I called for help, and you listened to my cry.

—*Jonah* 2:2

Chapter One

For a small gal she was a real firecracker. By the flash of those emerald eyes she looked ready to explode. And all because of him.

Watching her approach from her car, Trace Crawford swiped his Stetson from his head and prepared for the worst. It was no secret that he was the last person Paisley Norton would expect *or want* to find standing on her porch—his sentiments exactly.

He planted his boots and, as if to mock him, his spurs jingled cheerily—ha! Nothin' about the next few minutes promised to be cheerful.

There had been a time when he'd believed he had a pretty good head on his shoulders. Not anymore, and all of Mule Hollow was pretty much in agreement with that assumption. Applegate Thornton and Stanley Orr, the two old guys who hung out at Sam's Diner, letting everyone know their opinion about all things good, bad and just plum stupid, certainly did. They'd voted Trace's lapse in judgment as the "humdinger of all things *plum* stupid," to quote Applegate verbatim. And Trace was in total agreement.

He wished like nothing he'd ever wished before that he could take back having asked Paisley's cousin to marry him.

Sure, he'd been in a panic, but still, *what* had he been thinking?

You were thinking about your two-year-old niece. And how you didn't and still don't have any clue how to take care of her.

True. But still…how had he messed things up so bad?

"What are *you* doing here?" Paisley snapped, stepping onto her porch and edging past him.

Not wanting to give her the opportunity to slam her front door in his face, he scooted in front of her, trying to block her path. "I need your help," he said, causing her eyes to blaze with contempt. Her chin lifted.

"No!" The air vibrated with her anger. He started to speak but she pushed him in the chest and backed him up to the porch steps.

"It's not bad enough," she gritted out through perfect white teeth, "that I have to see you on the streets in town. Now you're trespassing on my property!" She yanked her arm up and pointed toward the road. "Get off. Go away. Or I'll call Brady."

Brady was the sheriff of Mule Hollow and a good friend. But in this instance Trace knew Brady would do his job and send him packing. And if this had been about himself alone, Trace would have stepped off that porch and been gone right then and there—he wouldn't have come here in the first place.

But this wasn't about him.

This was about his baby niece, and had been from the moment he'd first learned of her existence two months ago. Because she needed help he couldn't give her, and because he was all she had in the world, he'd proposed to this spitfire's cousin almost immediately…and that ill-fated proposal had caused all of this.

But there was no turning back now and she was going to listen to him. "I'm not going anywhere," he said firmly, knowing his eyes were flashing some steel of their own.

She glowered as her long-lashed eyes narrowed to slits.

"Look," he snapped, reining in his frustration, fighting to remain level headed and losing. Couldn't she see reason? Couldn't she at least listen instead of acting like Rambo in a skirt? "Zoey has gone through more than any little girl should have to go through. I don't care if you hate my guts— I *need* your help—"

"If you came to ask *me* to marry you, I'm going to punch you!"

"Marry you? Whoa, lady." His gaze slid down her battle-ready stance and he blurted out the first thing that came into his head: "That's the last thing I'd ever do."

The words were more of a reflex than anything. After all, popping that question had started all this trouble! He had no plans to make that mistake again. Especially with Paisley. It was safe to say she'd rather see him dragged across a patch of prickly pear cactus.

He was caught off guard when she paled, two bright spots of pink on her prominent cheekbones her only color.

"Th…then why are you here?" she asked, the green in her eyes swirling with a surprising vulnerability.

Had he embarrassed her? He had the impulse to back up and attempt to clarify his words, but he'd lost all confidence in his ability not to flub things further, so he plunged forward. Laying everything out in the open was the best option. "I came to offer you a job for the summer."

"A job," she scoffed. "*Me* work for *you?* Ha!"

No surprise there. He'd had the same reaction when the ladies in town had suggested Paisley was actually the perfect person for the job—how? But there were no other options. Even if Mule Hollow had an abundance of teenage babysitters, which it didn't, a teen wouldn't do in this instance. And for reasons he hadn't figured out, all the older ladies were unavailable. "Circumstances have left me without options." *So here I stand, not because I want to be, but because I must be.*

Suffocating weight settled over him, as if he had the whole world on his shoulders—and it was true. He had a little girl's world sitting squarely across both shoulders. "The social worker on my niece's case is coming out to make her final field visit and then finally I get custody of Zoey. I'm down to the wire here. I need to show I have someone reliable to care for her. I need someone to teach me what to do, because I have no clue."

Paisley's expression clearly said she would work for him the day pigs flew.

"Look," he said, rubbing the cramping muscles in his neck, "I get why you're staring at me like that. But the ladies said you needed a job and, well, you are a schoolteacher. When you aren't talking to me, you do seem like you can be a fairly nice person."

"Well, you're a charmer! A regular Don Juan."

No, he was an idiot! "I didn't mean it that way." He scrambled for the right words. "I'm sorry. Really, I am."

"Well," she snapped, her glare steamy, "at least you finally said something we both agree on. You most definitely *are* sorry."

Trace nodded. "I deserved that." She was right, after all.

He'd literally run her cousin out of town with his poorly thought-out proposal. "I get that you don't think much of me, but this is an innocent little girl we're talking about. And, the older ladies said that I've caused you to be in a financial bind since I am responsible for Rene leaving town."

Way to go, idiot. "I mean," he tried again, "they pointed out that you being a schoolteacher and having the summer off—well, you'd be the perfect person to help me and Zoey."

If his grandfather heard him right now, groveling, as he would have called it, the crusty old man would roll over in his grave. A man did not admit his shortcomings, especially to a woman. But all Trace could think of was Zoey and what a lousy guardian he would be. He had to get someone in his corner who knew about little girls—*really* knew about them. "I need someone to help care for her and teach me how at the same time."

His insides curled up thinking about the mess his widowed grandfather had made raising him and his sister alone. Trace knew he wouldn't do any better by Stephanie's daughter if he didn't get help with his newfound parenthood.

He still had a hard time realizing that his sister was dead. Or that she'd never bothered to tell him he was an uncle. He'd stopped trying to understand Stephanie a long time ago and had thought she'd hurt him as much as she possibly could. But the fact that she'd given birth and not contacted him…it cut deeper than anything she'd ever done. Anything his parents had ever done, either.

If Social Services hadn't found him he'd have never known about Zoey. And he'd have never had the chance to help her. *What were you thinking, Steph?*

Had his mixed up sister hated him so much that she'd rather her little girl believe she had no relatives at all?

His heart hurt at the thought. He'd regret for the rest of his life that he hadn't done more for Steph, but for Zoey things were going to be different. God had given him a second chance and he planned to do everything in his power to give that little girl a fair shot at life. Even if it meant begging the stubborn woman in front of him for her help. Taking a deep breath, he prayed silently for God to step into the equation and give him a hand. "Paisley, will you please help Zoey?"

For two months, *two months,* Paisley had been a big ball of anger and all because of this cowboy. *This* cowboy had ruined her and Rene's lifelong dream of settling down in a small town and raising their families together. He'd driven her cousin out of town—killing that dream with his callous insensitivity!

"This is preposterous," she said in disbelief, ignoring the desperation in his smoke-colored eyes. "I can't work for you."

Those smoky eyes mixed with his sand-colored curls and that chiseled jaw put the man in serious contention with good-looking country star Dirks Bentley. The combination of those boyish good looks and those unforgettable eyes had gotten them into this mess from the start. One look at him when she and Rene had walked into Sam's Diner and Rene had believed she'd fallen madly in love at first sight—it had taken several weeks before Trace even seemed to notice Rene. And then when he did start dating Rene, Paisley could tell there was no hope for the relationship. The man had been leading Rene on, but there was no convincing Rene of that…just remembering made Paisley's temperature rise.

"Please."

"No. No way, actually," she said. "You can't bring a child who needs to feel safe into a situation where two people dislike each other. What could you be thinking?"

"I know what you're saying, but I tried to find someone else and couldn't. Everyone already has commitments, while you have almost three months free until your teaching job starts. Zoey needs you."

Paisley had become a schoolteacher because she'd always had a heart for kids. And kids who'd been given a raw deal in life really cried out to her. Not that this gave the maddening man any excuse for hurting her cousin. Poor Rene had thought when he'd suddenly asked her to marry him that he'd fallen in love with her, too! It had been devastating for her to realize he was only looking for a mother for Zoey. Rene had felt bad for the little girl, but she'd been devastated by the knowledge that Trace wasn't in love with her and she'd left town...and poof, just like that, no more side-by-side houses or family backyard barbeques or playtime for their future kids. Nope he'd killed that. But worst of all...he'd hurt Rene.

"Please," he said. "I'm really sorry for hurting Rene. She didn't deserve the pain I caused her. But, my little niece doesn't deserve what's happened to her, either. Does she?"

Paisley had so many reasons to stay as far away from Trace as she could get—and then he touched her arm suddenly and every nerve ending in her body went on red alert. She yanked away from him, as if she'd just gotten tangled in an electric fence. To her horror her heartbeat sped up under his soulful gaze.

"No, she doesn't." It was true, despite her roiling emotions.

"I'll pay you a good wage," he added quickly. "I won't be around all that much—you know what it's like during the summer. Keeping a ranch the size of Clint Matlock's going is sometimes daylight to dark. But I'm going to try and not work so late every day. I've already talked with him and the foreman about needing to be home some."

She blinked as his words sank through the fog forming in her brain. *What was she thinking?* The man was basically asking her to work cowboy hours. But she did need the money, and there was the poor child, innocently doomed to his care…and *that* was the reason for her racing heart.

He'd latched onto his hat rim with both hands and his knuckles were white…seeing him suffer gave Paisley a moment of *great* satisfaction. She couldn't help pushing the issue. "You led Rene on," she snapped. "Do you know for a brief moment she thought you'd actually fallen head over heels in love with her—which is all she ever wanted."

No. No way could she work for this guy. Family loyalty mattered.

"I freaked out—I'm *sorry.* What more can I say?.Have you never messed up?"

Frustration and desperation edged his voice, and Paisley didn't feel the satisfaction she'd hoped for, but she didn't like him any less, either.

"Look, Rene is a great woman. The best," he continued in earnest. "She is. I respect her immensely and that's why I asked her to marry me—for Zoey's benefit. If that makes me a jerk, then I am. I fully admit it." He paused, holding her gaze. "But this jerk could really use some help, and if I have to grovel I will."

Shame infused Paisley. This macho, self-centered cowboy admitting for the sake of a little girl that he would grovel made her animosity toward him seem misdirected—selfish. It wasn't a good feeling.

Could she willingly ignore a child's need simply because of her own need for vindication?

She tried to harden her heart…but he'd hit her Achilles' heel. How could she ignore the child's needs? Her stomach rolled at the thought.

And then there was the fact that despite having her heart broken Rene was completely happy now…so did any of this matter to anyone but Paisley?

"I'll do it," she said, before she could change her mind. "For Zoey. *Not* for you in any way, shape or form. Is that understood?"

A smile exploded across Trace's handsome face and to her horror, before she'd even finished speaking, the crazy man grabbed her up in his strong arms and spun her around!

"Rene always said you were the best!" he whooped as they spun. "Thank you! Thank you! I promise you won't regret this."

Dizzy, angry and totally flustered she struggled against him. "Wh…whoa!" she sputtered, pushing against his broad shoulders, glaring down into his sparkling eyes, feeling his arms wrapped around her waist. "Put me down!"

At her command he dropped her like a rock. Feeling like she'd just fallen off the merry-go-round she stumbled away from him—most *assuredly* not merry! When he reached to steady her she held up a shaky hand of warning. "Stay," she snapped. She was so infuriated her pulse was pounding, her every nerve ending was sizzling with distaste.

"Rules," she gasped, breathlessly, glaring at him and the grin plastered across his face. "The ground rules are: *Don't* touch me. You got that, buster?"

Chapter Two

Big mistake. Big mistake. Big mistake.

The voice inside her head was getting on her nerves the next morning as Paisley parked her car in front of Sam's Diner—of course her nerves were shot, so it didn't take much. But, as she stepped onto the weathered planks of the sidewalk, the droning tone was as relentless as the midsummer sun that beamed down on her. She glanced down the street at the town she'd started to call home, needing the happy feeling she always got when she looked at the welcoming place.

Mule Hollow was a darling town of clapboard buildings lining the main street. It had been painted in an array of bright colors, highlighted by bright trim, giving it a very welcoming façade made more so by the window boxes that overflowed with assorted flowers. Amazing, simply amazing, she thought as always when she looked at it. The community had taken a dusty, dying town and done the ultimate makeover. It was simply the most welcoming place she'd ever seen...but even it wasn't making her happy this morning.

Walking into the diner, she still couldn't believe that starting Monday she would be working for Trace. *Big mistake—what would Rene think about it if she knew?*

Her cousin was now happily married to Clay Preston— they were on their honeymoon this very moment…she tried to counter her conscience. It wouldn't matter.

Maybe. Problem was, Paisley couldn't shake the feeling that this might present an uncomfortable situation.

Paisley pushed open the heavy swinging door and entered the rustic diner. A relic from days gone by but much loved by all who frequented it. A group of cowboys were in her way, paying their bill, so she moved over to her favorite table at the window.

"Good morning, Applegate and Stanley," she said, loudly. The two old men were hard of hearing and even harder on each other during at their daily checkers game. They seldom missed a day at the window table.

The diner was the hub of the town and Paisley enjoyed having coffee and pancakes here on Saturday mornings. She found something comforting about seeing everyone who came in and out, especially these two crusty old men with hearts as soft as marshmallows.

"Mornin' to you, too," App grunted, not looking up from the board. He always seemed to have a perpetual frown creasing his thin wrinkled face as he concentrated on his next move.

Stanley, the slightly plump teaser of the two, beamed at her. "Don't mind him. He ain't got nowhere ta go, so he's crabby. He needs ta surrender."

App shot his buddy a glare. "You wish, ya old coot."

Stanley tapped his watch face with his index finger.

"We gotta be at play practice in three hours, and at the rate you're goin', you ain't gonna have made this move before we have to quit."

Paisley had been just as surprised as everyone else when these two had volunteered to help run the sound and lights of the summer stock theater that one of the couples had opened. But what had been more shocking was that they were really good at it despite their hearing problems and their constant picking. "Hang in there, Applegate," she chuckled. "I have faith in you." She winked at Stanley, who plopped a handful of sunflower seeds into his mouth and grinned smugly.

She held a deep fondness for these two fellas in part because they'd been very good to Rene. Rene hadn't had an easy life. While Paisley had gone off to college and gotten her degree, her cousin had gladly put her life on hold and taken care of her invalid mother for years until her death a few months back. When Paisley had been hired as a substitute teacher for the last half of the year at the rural school Mule Hollow shared with another small town, she'd talked Rene into coming with her. The tiny town sounded like the perfect place to make their childhood dreams come true.

Having been tied down for years with her mother's home care, made working in the diner extremely good for Rene…with the exception that her infatuation with Trace Crawford had begun here.

Grudgingly, Paisley understood the attraction—even with her dislike of the cowboy, she couldn't deny that Trace was handsome. Okay, gorgeous! One look from those dreamy eyes and what woman's pulse wouldn't kick it up a notch?

Which explained her reaction to him yesterday. She

refused to even think for an instant that attraction was involved. The very idea was revolting, after the way he'd treated Rene.

"Paisley! Yo-hoo. Over here."

Relieved for the distraction from her disturbing thoughts, Paisley caught Esther Mae's wave from a booth near the kitchen where she sat with her two co-conspirators. The sixty-something dynamo with a fondness for brightly colored velour jogging outfits patted the bench beside her.

The herd of cowboys were exiting the building in a flurry of clinking spurs and clomping boots. Once they were out of the way, she crossed the room and slid into the booth. "Hi, ladies. We need to talk," she said, without any preamble. With these three a person had to get right down to business, because they were born matchmakers and she knew a setup when she saw it.

These three ladies had "helped" several women find their soul mates. But if they thought for one minute that Trace and she…no, they just better not be thinking in that direction.

"So why did you tell Trace I needed a job?" she asked, regarding each lady with a pointed look. "He might have fallen for the 'there was no one else with the time to help him' bit, but I'm not that naïve." These women gave of their time freely, helping everyone out in any way needed. There was no way they wouldn't have made especially certain this little, orphaned girl was well cared for. Which could only lead to one conclusion.

"So, did you take the job?" Norma Sue Jenkins asked, ignoring Paisley's probing. She was a robust cattlewoman and her husband was the foreman of Clint Matlock's ranch—the largest one in these parts and the ranch for which Trace worked. Beneath the denim overalls beat a heart of gold…and a steamroller personality.

And that was what worried Paisley. "Yes, I took the job. But if you three are getting any ideas about me and Trace, then stop it right now. I'm helping him because I need the job and someone needs to look out for Zoey."

Adela smiled. "We knew you would, dear. You have a wonderful heart." A wisp of a woman, she had sparkling blue eyes so clear a person thought she could see right through them. "You are a God-given opportunity for this tiny family."

"That's right," Esther Mae chimed in. "These last few months, since your cousin left town, you've been so miffed at Trace that you've been wound tighter than my Sunday girdle!"

"Esther Mae," Applegate snorted from the front window. "If yor gonna be tellin the world about yor girdle, then give a man time ta turn off his hearin' aid!"

"You go right ahead and turn that hearing aid off! You and your selective hearing," a pink Esther Mae huffed, then leaned in and whispered, "I guess that *was* a little out of line for a public place. But you know what I mean, girls."

"Amen to that," Norma Sue grunted. "You wouldn't ever catch me trying to get in one of those elastic body bands."

Despite her determination to be firm, Paisley chuckled. "You know very well why I've been so upset with him. He *ran* Rene off!"

"Yes, we understand your anger. But the poor man didn't really mean to hurt her," Adela said.

"Still, he did and I'm not going to forget that…however, I am going to work for him for the summer. In all good conscience, I can't *not* do it, since I really do have the time."

Sam came over and set her plate in front of her. The diminutive man didn't even bother to ask her what she wanted anymore. He just started cooking pancakes the minute she walked through the doorway on Saturday mornings.

"Here you are, Paisley," he said. "And you listen to my Adela. She's been praying about this ever since that boy found out he was get'n that little girl."

Paisley's heart fluttered at the love in his eyes when he smiled at Adela. Oh, to have a man love her like Sam loved Adela.

"I've been praying, too," Norma Sue said. "And I have a good feeling you being there to steer Trace in the right direction is a good thing. Men don't know nothin', and if you haven't noticed, he's really shook up about it. More than most. There's something about the boy that makes us wonder about what kind of past he's had."

"Look," Paisley said, setting the syrup down with a thud. Talking about Trace's past made her uncomfortable. "I'm not interested in the man's past. My only concern is helping Zoey."

Three pairs of eyes blinked at her in complete disbelief.

"*Really.* Ladies, surely y'all understand that I'm doing this for Zoey. If not for her I'd let the man sink—that means I don't want any crazy matchmaking ideas." More blinks, but they at least kept silent. "No pushing," she warned, not getting a good vibe at all.

She'd been blunt—not that it had done any good. Oh, no. They didn't look as if they'd heard a word she'd said. They were trying too hard to look innocent.

Ha!

"And besides," she said, deciding to take a different route. "I have serious concerns about how healthy it will be to bring a child into a house with two people who clearly dislike each other."

"Oh, now," Esther Mae sighed. "It's not as bad as all that. I think y'all are just out of sorts. Y'all would make a *grand* couple. Just think what pretty babies you'd have."

"What?" Paisley gasped.

"And speaking of Trace," Norma Sue said, looking past Paisley toward the door. "That is one fine looking cowboy. He looks like a weight has been lifted off his shoulders since I saw him yesterday. Just look at the spring in his step and the light in those gorgeous eyes. How could you even think about saying no to the man?"

"Good grief," Paisley muttered as she twisted toward the door.

Trace had stopped to say hello to App and Stanley before heading their way with that killer smile in perfect place. Her stomach turned queasy just looking at him—of course it was nothing more than nerves. Knowing she'd committed to work for him for the next few months made her want to toss her pancakes. No doubt about it: she had a bad case of dread.

"Good morning, ladies," he said, entirely too pleased with himself. "Did Paisley tell you she's agreed to rescue me?"

"I'm not rescuing you," she snapped, setting her fork down with a clatter. Food on an upset stomach would not be a good idea.

"You are rescuing me," he reiterated, firmly. "You have no idea. I actually *slept* last night."

"Oh, that is just so sweet," Esther Mae cooed. "Did you hear that, Paisley? The poor boy hasn't been sleeping, he's been so worried about how he was going to take care of that precious, precious child."

Of course she'd heard. And Paisley had to admit being that worried about Zoey was sweet.

"I hoped I'd find you here," he said, settling grateful eyes on her. "I went by your house first."

"Why?" she asked, more than a little aware of the looks passing between her obnoxious booth buddies—she felt like she was being offered up like a prize on the *Price Is Right,* for crying out loud!

"I took the day off and hoped you might go with me to pick out some things to make Zoey's room nice. You know, girly."

"What a *lovely* idea," Adela said.

"I don't—" she started, but gasped when Esther Mae elbowed her in the ribs.

"Sure, she'll go," the dastardly redhead exclaimed. "It's for the child."

Holding her ribs, Paisley glared from Esther to Norma Sue, hoping for some backup.

What she got was a thumbs up. "Sure, she'll go," the steamroller said, again plowing right over any ideas Paisley had of Norma helping her out.

Paisley rubbed her ribs and slumped in defeat. The awful truth was they were right—she needed to make certain Zoey's room was safe for her. She let out a slow breath. "I'd be happy to go," she said through clenched teeth. Resolved to her plight, she reached for her purse and stood up. "After all, we wouldn't want you decorating Zoey's room in hay bales and cowbells now, would we?"

"Nope," he said, totally unaffected by her sarcasm. "We wouldn't want that at all. Wait," he said, zeroing in on her plate. "You can finish your pancakes. You haven't taken a bite."

She dropped her money on the table and glared at the three wretched women smiling up at her. "I've lost my appetite. And besides," she said, giving him her attention, "we've got something much more important to do."

"See y'all later," Norma Sue and her cohorts called in chorus as Paisley stormed toward the exit. They would think what they wanted, so she couldn't worry about that. Focusing on the little girl was all she could do. It was the only thing that would help her get through this fiasco!

"Allow me," Trace said, beating her to the door despite her hurry.

She cut her eyes at him when she had to brush past. With him practically standing in her way she couldn't help noticing the totally masculine aftershave he wore.

"Thank you," she said, with a curt nod. As far as she was concerned he was a skunk to some extent and she would do well to remember that even if he didn't smell like one.

"Any time," he said, giving her a knowing smile. The rat knew—he couldn't possibly not know—how much she was hating this whole idea. He beat her to the truck door and opened it for her also—the double rat! All the manners in the world wouldn't change what he'd done to Rene.

She climbed into the truck, ignoring his offered hand and stared straight ahead as he closed the door. She stilled her emotions and watched him with cool eyes as he jogged around the truck and climbed behind the wheel. Being all torn up wasn't doing her any good. It was time for business. She needed to know what specifically she was dealing with.

"Why don't we run by your place and let me look at the house so I can see what we need to pick up today?" Her voice vibrated slightly, but considering the situation, she was pleased with herself.

"Sure," he said, backing the truck out of the parking space. "Sounds like a good plan."

Boy was he wrong, she thought, staring straight ahead. Nothing about *this* sounded like a good plan. Nothing at all.

Chapter Three

"Did you hear me?"

"What?" Trace realized Paisley had spoken. "Um, no, I'm sorry. What did you say?"

They were standing in what would be Zoey's room. It wasn't much to see, just a bunch of secondhand furniture that had been left in the house when he'd bought it. But he wasn't thinking about the furniture. He was lost in thought thinking about Paisley's eyes. No longer flashing anger, those fiery eyes had become distant and as cool as the Frio River—and it was a problem.

Every time she looked at him with those flat eyes he had the urge to rile her up so the fire he'd grown used to seeing would come dancing back!

Crazy. Plain stupidity was what it was.

But now, seeing her eyes spark with a little impatient irritation—sick man that he was, his pulse kicked up. He was losing it, no doubt about it.

"I asked what your ideas were for this room."

The room—*focus, man!* He blurted out the first thing that came to him. "Pillows." *Girls liked pillows, didn't they?*

Paisley eyed him suspiciously and then nodded. "Yes. Pillows are good. Not too many, though. She might have allergies. You did ask if she had allergies, didn't you?"

A sinking feeling hit him. "I didn't know I was supposed to." He hadn't asked much of anything. "Do you think she'll have them?"

Her eyes narrowed accusingly. "I guess they would have informed you of medical needs whether you asked or not."

"Yeah. Hopefully." A good parent—a responsible parent—would have immediately asked if Zoey had any medical problems.

Paisley's expression said she agreed with him whole-heartedly. "I've seen enough. I'm ready if you are," she said and was out the door like a woman on a mission.

With feet of lead he followed. She had no idea how *not* ready he was for any of this…and four hours later, pushing a buggy through a large chain store, he wasn't any more ready. Watching as she threw all kinds of colorful items in he was more uncomfortable and inept feeling than ever.

"You see, all of these curtains and even this sparkly material I'm buying for decoration are washable," she informed him, and then, like she'd done over and over again, she immediately headed off in search of her next find.

The woman had a plan and she was working it. No hesitation. No second guesses. And as she did it, she kept her distance, only talking to him when needed. Hitting him with those cool, assessing eyes when she did speak to him…and it was starting to add to his already stressed out nerves.

But he could handle it, he told himself. It meant if she applied the same diligence from shopping to her job, then Zoey—and he for that matter—was in great hands. The woman could concentrate like nothing he'd ever seen, and he liked that about her. As he rounded the corner, Paisley had just stepped onto a rickety shelving unit to reach for a lamp from the top shelf. The entire shelving unit—four rows of lamps—wobbled!

"Hey," he protested, springing forward. "What are you thinking?" he demanded, just as the unsteady lamp toppled, heading straight for her. He dove, snagged her around the waist and swung her out of its path.

"Put me down!" she exclaimed, kicking him in the shin! "I told you, no touching."

He caught the lamp—no thanks to her—and growled, "Cut it out." It felt like his college football days all over again. "You didn't have to kick me! Can't you see I was only saving your neck?" He glared down at her and, despite his throbbing leg, he chuckled. The woman was something…and all the fire was back in her eyes in a blaze of glory.

Her heart pounded erratically against his and her eyes narrowed. Clearly she was not happy about being held so close. Of course his chuckling didn't help, but he was captivated by the feel of her in his arms. Her eyes suddenly flickered to his lips!

His arms reacted all their own, tightening around her instantly. For a moment he couldn't move.

"Put me down."

Her clenched-teeth demand sliced through his insanity, and he lifted his gaze to meet cold eyes.

"I told you—no touching."

He set her on her feet, pronto, and stepped away.

"I could have gotten that," she huffed, as her green eyes popped against her now rose-glow complexion.

She was dynamite. Call him stupid, but he grinned. He couldn't help it. The woman was cute as all get-out when she was mad. And yes, he'd thought about kissing her. She had been in his arms looking up at him. It had been a totally natural reaction. One he'd put the brakes on immediately. He might find her attractive, but kissing her…that was out of the question.

"What are you smiling for?" she demanded.

"I'm sorry," he said. "But when you're mad your eyes do this great fire-and-flash thing. It's really cool."

"*It's cool?* You make me mad, grab me up when I told you no touching and then you say it's cool! Who do you think you are?"

"Hey now, just a blamed minute," he said, making a timeout sign with his hands. Sure, he shouldn't have grinned or thought all that other stuff, but she was out of line. "Look, you're the one stomping around barely speaking to me. If you'd just asked me to get that lamp in the first place, I wouldn't have had to save you from bringing it crashing down on your head." He looked at the lamp in his hand, as some sort of evidence.

Her lips flattened and he could tell she was holding back a zinger. But to her credit she contained it. "You're right," she said instead, after a considerable pause.

The admittance didn't make him feel good, though. The woman really thought he was a number one jerk. *The* number one jerk. "Look," he said, gauging his words. He was at risk of running her off and he could see it. "In the future, since you're going to be at the house and all, if you need me to do something, just ask." He gave a small smile of encouragement and worried he shouldn't have when she frowned. He had to try and get her past the anger she felt toward him.

"C'mon," he said, striving to sound lighthearted. "We've got things to buy and then you've got to show me what in the world to do with all this stuff. I'm clueless."

She was waffling, he could tell as her expression softened—she was a sensible woman, after all. She was a teacher, for goodness sakes. He gave her an encouraging smile, his hopes rising. And then he did it…what came natural to him under usual circumstances; he gave her a good ole Texas wink—*oh, man!*

"You just winked at me," she said. "Of all the unbelievable nerve."

"I didn't mean to. I'm sorry—"

"Oh, so you're telling me you had something in your eye."

"No, nothing's in my eye. I just winked at you. It didn't mean anything. Really, it didn't."

Paisley could not believe this man! Spinning away she stormed down the aisle, needing space. The squeak of the buggy wheels told her he was following her. At the checkout counter she started pulling things out of the buggy and tossing them on the conveyor belt. She couldn't unload things fast enough! The man was now *flirting* with her? Wasn't that what the winking was all about? And he'd grabbed her—*twice*.

Sure she'd knocked that lamp off the top shelf, but really, grabbing her and yanking her up against his chest was totally uncalled for. Totally!

"You okay, honey?" the middle-aged checker asked.

Paisley snatched a bottle of shampoo from the buggy and smacked it onto the counter with a thud. "I'm fine," she muttered, glancing at the woman's name tag. "Evelyn," she said more calmly. None of this was Evelyn's fault, so she didn't deserve to be treated badly.

Evelyn cut sharp eyes at Trace. "You ought to be. That's one fine-looking man you got there."

Paisley's mouth fell open. "Oh, no. No way. He's not my man." She shot Trace a glare that dared him to speak. He didn't. He just gave Evelyn that winsome smile, which made Paisley's temperature soar another notch.

Evelyn, on the other hand, grinned at him and sighed heavily as she grabbed an item and dragged it across the scanner without looking at it. How could she? Her eyes were glued to Trace.

"Oh, brother," Paisley muttered, returning to snatching things out of the buggy and throwing them on the counter. The man just looked at women and they lost all common sense!

"Made you mad, did he?" Evelyn asked.

Paisley scowled at the nosey woman. She had no intention of discussing why she disliked Trace with a total stranger. This was the checkout line, after all. Sadly, the woman took her silence as agreement.

"It's a cryin' shame that most of the lookers are jerks," she said.

Finally someone agreed with her! What a sweet woman. "Isn't it, though," Paisley said, looking at Trace's befuddled expression as she grabbed the comforter, handed it to Evelyn and then snatched the lamp out of his hands.

Evelyn made a clucking sound and gave Trace the once-over again. "What do you have to say for yourself?"

Paisley almost laughed at the woman's over-the-top inquisition.

"Well, I've apologized. What's a guy supposed to do?" he said, probably shocked to find his smile hadn't quite worked out like he'd thought it would.

Evelyn cut him off with the total for the items, holding out her hand.

Trace scowled, dug out his wallet and handed over the cash. After a few seconds they were done and pushing the buggy out the door.

"Hold your ground, honey," Evelyn called after her, and Paisley couldn't help chuckling. It was one more ridiculous moment to add to an altogether bizarre experience so far.

"So what was that all about?" Trace asked as soon as they reached the truck.

Paisley opened her door and climbed in without even offering to help him unload the bags. "Women as a whole don't like to be stepped on. We tend to stand together on issues like that." She went to yank the door shut, but he grabbed it and held fast.

"You aren't going to let this go, are you?"

"No. You're the kind of guy who thinks a cute smile and a wink will get you whatever it is that you want. I take offense at that kind of an attitude. Evelyn agreed."

She expected a comeback but got only a thoughtful stare from his stormy-weather eyes. After a couple of pulse beats he closed the door and finished loading the bags in silence. When he walked around to his side of the truck and climbed in, he still didn't say anything.

And all the way home he remained silent. Good, she thought. Maybe something she'd said had gotten through to him. You couldn't walk all over a woman's feelings and then expect a puny apology to fix things.

No matter how good-looking a man you were.

"Look, I know you dislike me. I know you don't think highly of me. And I know all the way back to town you've been sitting over there deciding to quit."

They were still sitting inside the truck, which he'd just pulled to a stop at the back of his house. They'd ridden the hour from Ranger to Mule Hollow in silence. Paisley had needed the silence. Now she leveled serious but calm eyes on him.

"That would mean Zoey would be left hanging...and we both know *she* doesn't deserve that."

"But I do," he said, and smiled.

"If the shoe fits. And I didn't say that to make you smile. Do you ever take anything seriously?"

"Oh, I'm serious. I'm smiling because you're staying to help me with Zoey. Thank you. That's my sole focus. You won't believe this but I'm nervous and it makes me react in stupid ways." He reached for the door handle. "I promise to try not to upset you anymore. Now, let's get to work. I have to move and dismantle the big bed that's in Zoey's room so I can set up her youth bed. That will keep me out of your way for a little while. How does that sound?"

"Great," she said, opening her door. She hopped out and helped unload the bags and carry them inside. On the porch was a large package with a UPS label on it.

"Youth bed," he said as he opened the screen and pushed the back door wide. He waited for her to lead the way inside.

She brushed past him hating the fact that when her arm touched his she felt like she'd stepped into a frying pan. Shocked again by how she reacted to his touch, she was thankful that he was staring at the package on the porch completely unaware of her. This time she couldn't blame the sensation of awareness on bad behavior on his part, which only made her more angry at him and furious with herself. She refused to acknowledge that the man could stir her senses. She refused to be another one of his easy targets.

"The youth bed was a good idea," she said, walking into the house and straight into the living room. There she dropped her bags on the couch. Trace brought the rest of the packages in and then took the UPS box to the back room and went to work. She did too.

On the trip back into town she'd had to do some major soul searching.

Positively Zoey needed someone in her corner other than her hopeless uncle. Maybe she was overreacting, but she was questioning everything about this job. One question weighed the heaviest on her mind. Was helping him gain full custody of his niece was really in the girl's best interest?

As she pulled furniture wax, pillows and an array of other items from their bags, the question plagued her. Working in the living room alone gave her the space to think. She sent a prayer up that the Lord would give her some kind of peace about what she was doing.

Chapter Four

Paisley soon realized that though Trace was out of sight, he wasn't out of mind and definitely not out of earshot. He was fond of Brooks and Dunn tunes but she had a feeling that if Kix and Ronnie heard his rendition of "Boot Scootin' Boogie" they might pay him not to whistle it!

She was seriously considering doing that herself. But she wouldn't, because, oddly enough, his whistle while-you-work attitude gave her some peace. It showed her that he was actually enjoying himself back there. As upset and angry at him as she was, there was no denying that the man seemed sincere about making things perfect for Zoey. Which reminded her why she'd gone to the store with him in the first place.

Paisley moved around the living room, waxing tables, resituating furniture and began cleaning out a chest she found in the corner. It would make a perfect toy chest. And all the while she worked she wondered about the man in the other room.

He seemed completely out of touch with the softer side

of life; his bare "bunkhouse" decorating style proved that, but he was determined to make it right for Zoey. And, despite everything, that was the reason Paisley hadn't completely given herself over to the fact that she was making a mistake helping him gain custody of Zoey.

Feeling more content with her decision, she worked diligently. There was a lot to be done before Zoey arrived.

She'd just draped the new, red throw over the back of the couch and walked into the kitchen when he came up the hall with the wooden headboard from the adult bed. Seeing that his arms were full, she rushed toward the back door to open it for him.

"Thank yo—" he said, but the words died midstream as his gaze locked on the living room over her shoulder. He set the headboard down with a thud. "Is that *my* living room?"

She fought a smile, really fought it because she didn't want to smile at that man. But the smile battled through and her lips turned up on both ends. How could she not smile? He was looking at her handiwork with the awe of a kid who'd just gotten his very first pony! His expression was so delighted that she turned to survey the room again. It was the same room, but the furniture now gleamed bright and smelled of lemon. She'd placed pillows and throws across the couch and a colorful rug, along with a couple of real plants. And in the corner she'd placed the small chest, now full of toys. In that same corner was a pint-size table with coloring books she thought Zoey might enjoy.

"I'm not finished, but I think it's looking cozy," she said, glancing up at Trace. Her shoulder was brushing his and she stepped slightly away, ignoring the way her skin tingled.

"Cozy. No joke! It's gone from looking like the inside of a tack room to a room that a little girl can be nurtured in."

Paisley turned to him. "I promise you, Zoey will be nurtured while I'm here." He looked pensive at her words.

"Please don't take that wrong. I didn't mean any disrespect to you."

"I didn't," she said. "I'm just saying you don't have to worry about that."

"Believe me, the one thing I'm not worried about is you," he said. "I know you'll do great by her. It's me I'm worried about. Honestly, I know all there is to know about taking care of a calf or a colt. You know, what they need in order to grow up strong and healthy. But a little girl…"

Touched, Paisley felt compelled to reassure him. "Relax. You'll do just fine." He didn't look too sure but picked up the headboard and walked away, giving her a small smile as he went. There was nothing flirtatious in the smile. It was more from uncertainty—nervousness. The man was a puzzle. She watched him far longer than she should have as he headed toward the barn. A puzzle she had no business wondering about, she reminded herself as she hurried back to work.

However, her thoughts weren't cooperating and went immediately to a small box of professional photos she'd found buried at the bottom of the chest she'd cleared out for Zoey's toys. They were several action shots of Trace competing at different rodeos. The fact that he'd hidden them beneath a trunkful of old horse magazines instead of hanging them on the wall made her think he wasn't as full of himself as she'd thought. Maybe.

She'd lain them on the coffee table, as if she'd been dealing cards, not sure what to do with them. Now she gathered them up and headed toward the kitchen and slid them into a drawer. But not before pausing to riffle through them again. He was riding bulls in several of the shots, and just looking at him on top of those animals made her heart stop. She had to admit that though she knew nothing about bull riding, he did look like he had everything under control. He was stretched back, one arm gripping the rope and the other flung out for balance. It was breathtaking and dangerous, and she couldn't seem to stop gawking at them. The other photos were of him doing what she thought they called steer wrestling. He was flinging himself out of his saddle going after the steer. In others shots he'd taken hold of the animal and was wrestling it to the ground by hooking his arms around the animal's horns, planting his boots and twisting. While these shots weren't so dangerous looking, they still showed Trace Crawford "the cowboy" off to perfection. He was agile, athletic and by the look on his face extremely dedicated to accomplishing the task at hand… and now, he was putting all that intense focus on making a home for a little girl who had no home or mother.

He *still* acted like a jerk too many times to count, but not where Zoey was concerned. Maybe it *was* nerves. Of course, nerves might be excusable in some instances, but that still didn't get him off the hook where Rene was concerned.

"Here she comes," Paisley said on Thursday. She and Trace were standing beside each other on the porch watching as a car turned into his drive. The man had very nearly paced a hole in the porch while they'd been waiting for Zoey to arrive.

The last few days had been busy as they'd transformed

his house into a home. The social worker, a Mrs. Reynolds, had come out on Tuesday and to his complete shock she'd given him the official nod—which paved the way for Zoey to arrive today. When Mrs. Reynolds gave him the news Paisley had never seen a man so relieved and surprised and scared in all of her life.

She'd been forced to spend much time with him, getting the house in order and she'd thought the seal of approval had helped him relax a bit. But watching him now, pacing a hole in his porch, she wondered if maybe she should have spent time getting *him* in order.

He looked petrified as he spun toward her. "Do I look all right? I mean, do I look —do you think she'll like me? I'm not going to scare her, am I?"

Even knowing how nervous he was, his statement was unexpected. "Of course you won't scare her," she said, then shocked herself by taking his hand and squeezing. "She is going to love you," she assured him. Not that it did any good. He still looked like he was about to go over the edge of a cliff as his gaze shifted back to the car stopping in the drive. Paisley let go of his hand and expected that he would walk off the porch to greet Mrs. Reynolds, but he didn't move.

Mrs. Reynolds hustled over to them, her arms pumping, and with the harried look of a woman with much to do and not enough time to do it.

"I have her things," she said in a rush. "If you'll unload the trunk while I get her out of her car seat that would be good. Remember that I said she is a quiet one. But I think with time she'll come out of her shell. Normally I would stay while she acclimates but I've had a call that I'm needed elsewhere. There is an emergency case. I'm going to take charge of several children." She spun and sped back toward the car.

"But aren't you going to stay long enough to help her settle in?" Trace called after her, finally moving as he followed with apparently lead-filled boots.

"You don't need me. Per my preliminary visit, you're prepared. Zoey is in very capable hands. And you have Miss Norton's help," Mrs. Reynolds rattled off over her shoulder. "Have no fear. You'll all settle in together."

He halted and looked back at Paisley, so alarmed she imagined him screaming, "What do you mean have no fear?"

"But I *do* need her," he said instead.

Paisley's brow furrowed. This was ridiculous! What was *wrong* with him? "Will you relax? She can't help it if she has to go. Kids need her more than you," she hissed under her breath, not wanting Mrs. Reynolds to hear. "It's going to be fine. Go unload the trunk and pull yourself together."

Grim faced he strode toward the trunk while she went to watch Mrs. Reynolds lift Zoey from her car-seat into her ample arms.

Zoey had long, sandy-blond ringlets that hung nearly to her shoulders and big, serious eyes that immediately reminded Paisley of Trace's. The clear hazel tone mingled with brown was so like his that Paisley would have known this was his niece or even his daughter if they'd been in a roomful of twenty children. She was darling.

Trace eased around the back of the car with a small suitcase in his hand and stopped dead in his tracks, staring at Zoey. His expression was heart wrenching, even to Paisley, as he took in the sight of his niece for the first time. He seemed to stop breathing, and in the bright sunlight the gleam of tears was unmistakable in his eyes. Paisley swallowed hard and felt tears pool in her own eyes. She was mesmerized by the emotions radiating off of Trace. She expected by his expression that he would swing Zoey into one of his exuberant hugs at any moment…only he didn't move. Instead he shifted lost eyes to Paisley.

In that instant Paisley realized that something was wrong. Really, *terribly* wrong.

All this time she'd put his actions off as a scared bachelor navigating the new waters of unexpected parenthood…yes, she'd believed he was going a little overboard with his reactions. But now, looking at his complete lockdown, she understood his fear went deeper than ever she'd expected.

Zoey was clinging to a rag bunny but looking at him with bright eyes. Paisley was afraid he was going to scare her after all.

"Zoey, this is your Uncle Trace," Mrs. Reynolds said, so intent on getting to the emergency case waiting for her that she was oblivious to the fact that she had one happening right in front of her. She stood the poor child on the ground and spoke to her like she was old enough at two years to understand what was happening to her. "Like I told you before, honey, you'll be living with him now. Isn't that wonderful?"

Trace set the case down but made no other move—at least he wasn't running away. Paisley willed him to say something, to reach out and give Zoey a hug. Or *at least* bend down to her level and say something to make her transition easier. It was evident in her face that she was growing more and more uncomfortable with the situation. Instead he just stood as rigid as a frozen flagpole.

Mrs. Reynolds' brow bunched, but she kept on trying. "Zoey, say hello to your Uncle Trace," she urged, more firmly.

"'Lo," Zoey murmured obligingly in a tiny voice that ripped at Paisley's heart.

Trace finally reacted! "Hi," he croaked, but he still didn't make a move!

Mrs. Reynolds glanced at her watch and then shut the door to the car. She was ready to leave. Paisley couldn't stand the look that flashed in Zoey's eyes as she stared at that closed door. It was as if she dreaded once more being left on this side of it with total strangers. Even at her age she understood that much.

A flashpoint of anger swept through Paisley, and unable to stand it any longer she stepped in and took charge of the deteriorating situation. It was similar to how she would have handled a child who wasn't ready to let go of a parent on the first day of school.

What in Trace Crawford's background would explain his behavior? Kneeling down to Zoey's level Paisley smiled warmly. "Hi, Zoey. I'm Paisley, and I'm going to be taking care of you. I think we are going to be great friends. What's your bunny's name?"

A flicker of warmth moved through her eyes as she glanced from Paisley to her rag bunny. Paisley ached to pull her into an embrace.

"Friend," Zoey said in her two-year-old voice as she held out the bunny. The word came out sounding more like *Fa-wind,* but it was clearly understandable. The bunny was her friend…her comfort, too, Paisley could see.

"What a perfect name," she said. "How about you, Friend and I go up to the house for cookies and milk? I'm going to be your friend, too, okay?"

Zoey shot a hesitant look Trace's direction, then nodded.

"Can I pick you up?" Paisley asked her and was relieved when the tot gave her another tiny nod. Paisley had wanted to give her a hug from the moment she'd seen her and now she did just that. And to her surprise Zoey hugged back and didn't let go, clinging to Paisley with more strength than she'd thought possible for a little girl. Holding her tight, Paisley stood up with her in her arms and shot the *statue* a scathing glare, but she kept her words light for Zoey's ears. "We are going for cookies while y'all get everything else figured out. How does that sound?" she asked Mrs. Reynolds, but at this point she wasn't really interested in what the woman or Trace had to say. She was here for Zoey and suddenly very thankful that God had brought her, even if it was kicking and screaming, into this situation.

"Perfect," the other woman gushed. "I'll leave here knowing I've left Zoey in capable hands."

"You can be sure of that," Paisley assured her and marched toward the house.

She could hear a baffled Mrs. Reynolds asking Trace if he was okay. Paisley couldn't hear his reply as she mounted the steps and opened the screen, but she would… he could count on that.

The man had *frozen*.

On one hand she was furious with him, but on the other she knew she'd seen real emotion in his eyes and knew he cared. There was more here than she'd realized when she took on this job, but you could bet the bank that she was going to get to the heart of the matter.

Chapter Five

Trace watched Mrs. Reynolds' car disappear out of sight. What was wrong with him! He'd just stood there. He was a real piece of work, standing there like an oaf.

But when he'd looked at her, holding her bunny…he'd seen *Steph*. It had been a slam in the gut, and all the air had gone out of him and he just hadn't been able to get it back. Zoey looked just like her mother had when she'd been that age. And not only had seeing the resemblance caused his trepidation to be all the more painfully present—it was as if he was looking at a fresh canvas. Perfect. Unflawed…like Steph had been when their life had fallen apart. He'd seen firsthand that when it came to his sister the portrait hadn't ended up pretty. He pushed the depressing thoughts away and trudged up the steps to ease open the door.

All his life he'd felt like he'd failed his big sister, and the fact that she'd kept Zoey from him said she thought he would fail her daughter, too. For months now the knowledge had been eating at him but it hadn't actually hit him until he saw Zoey. Steph may have known exactly what she was doing when she'd not told anyone about him—had felt like she was protecting Zoey from a similar upbringing as she'd had? Or could it simply have been for spite?

The questions plagued him as he set Zoey's suitcase in the hall and headed slowly toward the kitchen and the sound of Paisley's voice.

The one thing he knew for certain at the moment, the thing he had absolutely no questions about was that he owed Norma Sue, Adela and Esther Mae hugs of gratitude the next time he saw them! They had made the right call when they'd talked him into asking Paisley for help. Without her, a few minutes ago he'd have been doomed.

Pausing at the door, he took a deep breath to steady his nerves. For goodness' sake, his insides were more torn up than they'd been after being tromped on three years ago by an angry bull. That bull had crushed ribs, torn ligaments and bruised his spleen—it had been so bad Trace decided his bull riding days were over…and now to think a tiny tot could rival all of that. But it was true.

He stood in the hall and listened to what was being said in the next room as he tried to get himself ready to start this new life. Ready or not it was here.

"I like to dip mine," Paisley was saying.

There was no reply, but Paisley chuckled. The sound was pure and lovely and his heart lurched in his chest when it was answered by a very small giggle from Zoey. Trace grinned automatically at the sound. He thanked God again, sure that Paisley was not only going to save the day but save the entire situation. She gave him a sense of hope.

"Let's dip another one while we wait for your Uncle Trace. I *know* he's around here somewhere very close."

She was onto him. He took a breath and squared his shoulders—and prayed for help. God had sent him Paisley. Now if He would just send Trace wisdom and a voice of his own.

"There he is," Paisley said brightly, giving him a questioning glare as he rounded the corner—it brought him up short for a second. She might have saved the day, but he knew his reckoning was coming.

He crossed to the table and tried to smile, but his face felt stiff and his throat was about as dry as a dirt arena in August. But he would speak this time.

"Hi, Zoey," he said past the log lodged in his throat. She looked up at him from her chair and he felt like he was a giant looking down into her wide eyes. Paisley was sitting, too. He did what he'd seen Paisley do outside and dropped to one knee in front of Zoey. His arms ached to hug her, he felt so unworthy and she stared at him.

"Trace, guess what," Paisley said, cheerfully, drawing him to look at her.

"What?" he asked, seeing questions in her eyes.

"Zoey really likes hugs. She told me Friend does, too. How about you? Do you like hugs?"

He nodded, glancing at Zoey. In that instant, by the shy smile of a tiny little girl, he lost his heart irrevocably—which made his shortcomings all the more unbearable.

"I like hugs very much," he managed, but his voice cracked. This was his niece. His sister's child. His flesh and blood. "Can I hug you?" he asked, and Zoey held out her arms. Friend was dangling from one hand. Feeling like he'd never felt before, Trace leaned in and gently hugged her close. She smelled like chocolate chip cookies and milk mixed with the sweet scent of baby shampoo. Her curls tickled his nose as over her head he met Paisley's steadfast gaze. Her eyes were bright with unshed tears as he mouthed the words "thank you."

He owed her a debt of gratitude that he could never repay, and this was only the beginning. As he let go of Zoey and took the seat beside her he wondered what he was going to owe Paisley by the end of the summer.

The old fears crowded at the back of his mind like a herd of cattle trying to get through a closed gate. But he held fast and concentrated on the moment.

"Would you like your Uncle Trace to show you your room?" Paisley asked.

Zoey nodded and gave him a heart-melting smile.

He stood and lifted her out of the chair and set her on her sandal-clad feet. He thought about carrying her but decided not to. When she slipped her tiny hand into his and looked up at him with all the trust in the world his throat clogged up again and he felt like he'd just been kicked in the gut.

"Do you like to play with dolls?" he forced himself to ask but felt his forehead dampen. She nodded but didn't speak as they left the kitchen.

Paisley followed them down the hall, but halfway along he moved to the side. "You go in first," he told her. If the payoff for all her hard work was seeing the expression on Zoey's face when she walked into the room she'd created for Zoey, then he wanted Paisley to reap that reward. She certainly deserved it.

And he needed a second to get his bearings. He could do this. He was doing this. Paisley was here, helping, coaxing.

She smiled like she understood and swept past them. "Oh, thank you," she said, dramatically. "I can't *wait* to play!"

"Me, too," Zoey said with animation lighting her pixy face. She led the way into the room but stopped just inside the door and her eyes grew wider than pancakes. A gasp escaped her lips. He knew the feeling, he'd experienced it the night he'd come home and walked in after Paisley had worked all day decorating it. The curtains were pink and fluffy, the bedspread on the miniature bed was some kind of soft inviting fabric with sparkling threads running through it. The lamp Paisley had almost risked life and limb to buy was on the bedside, making little stars on the ceiling—how it did that in the daylight was a mystery to him, but they were there. And while all of this was wonderful, it was the corner of the room that held Zoey's attention. That was where the tent of shimmering material had been erected, and inside the large tented area were the dolls and all the things a doll could ask for.

Paisley's hand went to her heart as she saw the look of awe on Zoey's face.

Without hesitation Zoey walked inside the tent, laid her bunny in the tiny baby bed and fixed the covers around him. Then she sat down in front of the dolls, picking one up and then another.

Moving to stand beside Paisley, Trace couldn't stop himself from slipping his arm around her waist and squeezing—he needed the contact himself and hoped she wouldn't kick him. "I think she likes it," he said softly.

She looked up at him with misty eyes that took his breath. Suddenly a spark of challenge vaporized the moisture and she grinned mischievously. "Thanks," she said, slipping out of her sandals. "Now take your boots off, buster. It's time to play."

"Play?" he said in surprise.

She grasped his hand and pulled him toward the tent and asked, "You do know how to play, right?"

"With dolls?"

She nodded. "You have to play with dolls if you're going to be a daddy to a little girl."

Daddy. His feet planted themselves on the hardwood. "I don't know about playing dolls!"

"But you will," Paisley laughed. "Don't look so serious. This is going to be fun."

He was sweating bullets and seriously in fear that he was going to pass out, and she was telling him this was *fun.* "Fun," he croaked and swiped his forehead with his shirt-sleeve.

Paisley's brows dipped and she slipped her arm in his. "Men!" she said and yanked him forward. "Relax, macho man, you might enjoy it."

Chapter Six

"**Y**ou hold," Zoey said, pushing a doll into Trace's hands the second he sat down inside the tent.

He clumsily took the fat, rubber baby doll and the bottle Zoey thrust into his hands. When the child stood back and blinked big eyes at him, he looked so adorably lost—well…lost certainly. He was scared stiff.

Paisley had thought that giving him a few minutes to get his act together would help, and it had—for about a second. She felt as if she were running hurdles where he was concerned—she'd get over one hurdle and then another would be waiting.

"Put the bottle in its mouth," she instructed him. "Now *rock* the baby." Looking more like a father who'd just been handed his newborn infant than one handed a doll, he did as he was told.

Zoey watched as Trace put the bottle in the doll's mouth and gave her his best smile—that in itself was a plus. But Zoey didn't return the smile. Instead she gave him a crisp nod of satisfaction, turned to another doll and thrust that at Paisley, with a tiny baby blanket. Again she watched expectantly.

Paisley, hoping to reassure her, gently wrapped the doll in the blanket then cradled it close. "What a sweet baby you are," she said, rocking gently.

Zoey's lips curled up slightly at the ends and then, satisfied that her babies were taken care of, she scanned the other things inside the canopy. Spotting the tiny red rocking chair, she daintily sat down and proceeded to watch them with serious eyes.

Trace looked at Paisley like a lost puppy. One minute she wanted to strangle the man and then she wanted to put her arms around him and tell him everything was going to be all right.

Boy, was that not happening! Not happening at all!

"Zoey is getting used to us, I think," she said instead, focusing. The little girl's quietness worried her some, but she didn't say that just yet. She honestly didn't think Trace could handle anything but encouragement.

"Don't you want to rock a baby?" she asked, but Zoey shook her head emphatically.

"Then you rock and we'll take care of the babies. Right, Uncle Trace?"

Trace's forehead creased and his jaw tensed more—if that were possible. She nodded at him, willing him as she'd been doing from the first moment to add something encouraging to the conversation. He *had* to participate. He had to loosen up.

"Yeah," he said finally. "We'll rock them." He proceeded to rock the doll, causing Paisley to bite back a chuckle. The man needed guidance, and the doll was going to need traction.

She couldn't take it anymore. She needed to talk to Trace and poor Zoey had to be tired, so Paisley decided it was time for a lullaby and began softly singing. Zoey didn't need much encouragement to fall asleep. Almost instantly she crawled from the chair and snuggled down beside the dolls on the soft blanket. Paisley gently smoothed her hair and patted her back.

The minute her eyes closed, Trace was out of the tent and out of the room.

He didn't even wait for Paisley to get up.

This man…the same man whose pictures in the drawer testified that he rode thousand-pound, rampaging bulls with the finesse and ease of a master! Could he truly be terrified of a little girl coming into his life, or was there more?

It was time for answers.

She found him on the front porch pacing like a high school basketball coach. He was rubbing the back of his neck, like she'd realized he did when he was stressing. The instant she closed the door he swung toward her.

"What was I thinking?" he growled and resumed pacing. "Did you *see* how she was looking at me? She's an innocent little girl—what do I know about raising a little girl? She's going to need special care. She's going to need guidance. She's gonna need things I can't give her! What an idiot—"

"Stop!" Paisley snapped and stepped in front of him. "What is your *problem?*" she asked. "It is terribly obvious something more serious than new-daddy jitters is going on here. Don't you think it's time to clue me in?"

He swallowed hard but instead of opening up he turned deep eggplant and stalked off the porch toward the barn.

"Wait, Trace!" she called, jogging after him. When he kept plowing forward she grabbed his arm, intending to swing him around to face her, but he was so intent that she just ended up being pulled along beside him. "Something is up with you," she said, stumbling to hang on to him, determined to get him to talk. "I don't know what it is, but I do believe I deserve an answer. You hired me to help. How can I help if I don't know the score? It's time to come clean to me about why you have been in such a panic since the day you found out you were getting this sweet little girl."

He stopped at the corral and stared at the mare and newborn colt inside. Tension radiated from every rigid line of his body. Paisley's heart was jumping against her ribs, and without another thought she let go of his arm and placed a hand between his shoulder blades and rubbed soothingly. His muscles bunched beneath her palm and he sucked in a deep breath.

"Talk to me," she urged.

It was unseasonably hot for the last week of May and the afternoon sun beat down on them. It did nothing to compare to the heat in Trace's eyes when he suddenly swung around to look at her. Raging hot anger glared back at her.

"I *can't* do this," he gritted out. "What was I thinking?"

Paisley took a step back as if he'd slapped her. The gutless whiner! She'd been feeling sorry for the guy, but this— this wasn't happening. "I don't know what your problem is, buddy, but this pity party you have going on has to stop."

"Pity party?" Disbelief rang in his voice. "Is that what you think this is? Believe me, it's not for me but for her. For having to live with me, a man who has no way of giving her the guidance she is going to need to become a good woman. Stephanie was right not to let me know about her daughter. Zoey would have been better off in foster care—"

The last words were barely audible and they tore at Paisley with the earnest honesty of them. He truly believed he was going to fail Zoey—what was up with that? "I hadn't expected this out of you," she snapped. "Why do you insist on defeat when you've only just begun?" She wanted to grab him by the collar and shake him, but instead she put her fists on her hips and stared at him.

"Please don't shout. You'll wake Zoey up and I'm not ready," he said in all seriousness.

"Start talking or I will shout," she warned, though she really wouldn't have. Zoey didn't need to see him like this, either.

He rubbed his neck and then leaned back, one booted foot propped against the steel pipe rail of the corral. He took another deep breath, as if marshalling his thoughts.

He made a stunning portrait, like the cover of a book or a country western music CD. He was beautiful—in a completely manly way. But the man had to have more inside him than just this appealing outer shell...he had to.

"Look, despite the fact that I don't like you much, somewhere along the way I've started rooting for you. For Zoey's sake," she amended, so he wouldn't get the wrong idea. "C'mon Trace. Give me something so I can help you."

His shoulders slumped and he looked like talking was the last thing he wanted to do. "My dad was a rodeo bum."

The words were flat. Apologetic. As if it was his fault his dad was any kind of bum.

"He left when I was about Zoey's age and my sister was not quite five. Very soon after, my mom drank herself into an early grave and left us to be raised by my mother's widowed father."

"I'm sorry," Paisley said. "That must have been hard."

"Yeah, you could say that. My granddad was a bitter man who didn't have a clue how to raise kids...especially girls. Poor Steph didn't stand a chance. And I didn't help her much. I'm the last person Zoey needs."

This revelation gave her a glimpse into his heart, exposing how deep-seated his fear was, and she felt true compassion for him. "I hate that that happened to you, but that doesn't explain why you are acting the way you've been acting. You walked in Zoey's shoes. You know exactly how she feels, but more importantly what she *will* feel as she grows up. Don't you see that you're exactly the right person to help her?"

"Not really. I was two years younger than my sister, and I watched as she rebelled against everything my grandfather did. Why shouldn't she?" he asked, sweeping his hat from his head and setting it on his thigh. "The poor girl was made fun of for years because of her clothes or her hair— what did Granddad know about fixing a little girl's hair up nice? Nothing. He didn't know anything about anything else either. Girls need guidance, understanding…Steph had none of that. In the end she turned to drugs and alcohol and we lost her."

So he'd been about two years younger than his sister and he'd felt helpless. "You were the younger child. You couldn't make choices for her."

"But I can for Zoey. I can't let history repeat itself with her."

He closed his eyes and leaned his head back against the top rail of the high corral. Paisley studied the sandy lashes against his tanned skin. His lips were clamped firmly together in resolute worry, and she could hardly stand it— she suddenly wanted to see those lips smile that goosepimple-producing smile of his…crazy inappropriate ideas!

"Trace Crawford," she snapped, a bit harder than intended, fueled by her anger at herself as much as him. "God doesn't make mistakes. He put that little girl into your care." She flung her arm behind her, pointing toward the house where Zoey slept. "I don't know why you had the childhood that you had. I don't know why your sister had to suffer or choose the path that she chose, nor do I know why your parents chose the path that they took. But what I do know is that when given notice that you had a niece, you didn't hesitate—even with the fear inside of you, you chose to step up to the plate. I really am only now beginning to get to know you, but so far…" she hesitated as the truth hit her. "So far, I admire you for what you've done. Now all you have to do is grab the proverbial bull by the horns and get on with it. Do you get my drift?"

He'd opened grave eyes and was studying her but said nothing as if she hadn't gotten through his thick head.

Paisley scowled. "Don't you get it? That little girl is yours. Period. It's a done deal. There's no going back. She can't help her background and you can't help yours. But you are all each other has, so get used to it."

He continued to stare at her, and finally the corner of his lip lifted ever so slightly and the smoke in his eyes shifted like sun peeking through gray clouds. "You are one tough cookie, Paisley Norton," he said, finally. "Do you know that?"

"I work hard at it," she snapped. He had no idea just how determined she could be.

He laughed unexpectedly. It was a laugh full of tension and release all tangled together. Conflict and hope that there was hope. "So," he said after the chuckle died a quick death and he turned serious again, "you think I can do this?" The question was quiet.

"With God's help."

"And yours?"

The way he said the question, the way he looked at her as he asked, caused a warm tightening in her chest. Her heart slowed…then surged unusually. "For a while," she said, bewildered by the feeling. She swallowed and continued, "But I'll be leaving at the end of the summer and God will still be with you. He's much more important than I am to the success of Zoey's life."

He straightened to his full height and put his hat back on. She watched, feeling oddly off-kilter, while he seemed calmer, his strain slackened.

"I think you're shooting your role in this way too short, Paisley. If you hadn't been here, I'd have already turned tail and run clean to Mexico."

Paisley couldn't tear her eyes away from his. "You wouldn't ever turn tail and run from anything. Especially a little girl who adored you the instant she saw you."

"Do you really believe that?"

She nodded. "Yeah, actually I do."

"I'm going to need you," he said quietly holding her gaze.

Her heart was pounding. "I'm right here," she said. And she was. For her, just like for him, there was no turning back. God had put her here for Zoey…and maybe to change this knucklehead's outlook in the process.

Chapter Seven

"How did your day go?" Trace asked the next evening as soon as he climbed out of his truck and walked into the house. He was covered in a thin layer of dust, and by the way his T-shirt clung to his torso it was obvious it had been through a hard afternoon in the sun.

Paisley crinkled her nose. "It was more pleasant than yours and far more agreeable smelling."

"That's a good thing." He grinned and tugged at the neck of the tee. "I've been in the saddle, soaked most of the day, so it's a wonder you can stand this close. I'm on my way to clean up. Where's Zoey?"

Paisley crooked her finger and led the way down the hall to Zoey's room. She placed a finger to her lips then they peeked around the corner. Zoey was playing in her tent with her dolls.

"Wow, she's talking to them," Trace whispered in her ear as they backed away and went back to the kitchen. Once there he beamed. "She looks more comfortable."

"She's getting there. We read and colored and played all day. I think she's adapting. She even asked where Uncle was."

"No kidding?"

Paisley laughed, seeing the delight on his face. "No, really. You were a hit yesterday." It was true. Zoey awakened from her nap grumpy and had hidden behind the couch in the living room. When they'd tried to pick her up she'd started screaming. Of course that had terrified Trace. Though Paisley wanted to intervene she'd held back, watching to see how Trace would handle himself. After all, she wasn't going to be here for the night, and if Zoey awakened he'd be alone dealing with whatever happened. Her heart had ached as he'd stooped to Zoey's level and talked soothingly to her. He reassured her that he loved her and said she could come out from behind the couch when she was ready and wanted to play.

The man had then begun treading a rut across the kitchen floor as he waited for Zoey to come out from behind the couch. Paisley had tried to ease his worries by talking to him as she began fixing dinner. She'd decided since she loved to cook this would be part of her job description. It also gave her something to focus on other than the impulse to reach out and hug the man's worries away every time he paced past her!

They'd both been relieved when Zoey had eventually come into the kitchen. "Come color," she had said, taking Trace's hand as if nothing had happened. With those two simple words the rest of the afternoon had gone easier.

Paisley, on the other hand, had to admit that her anger at Trace had disappeared for the most part. True, she thought he'd been in the wrong, but understanding the circumstances made it hard to keep up the fight.

She'd spent most of her evening thinking about him and Zoey, and she'd prayed God would help her help them.

And when thoughts of how momentarily attracted she'd been toward him during their talk had surfaced she'd forced them aside and refused to acknowledge them.

"I think I'll hurry and get that shower," Trace said, drawing her back to the moment. "I want to play with her before supper."

"I think that's a very good idea," Paisley said, busying herself with tossing the salad.

"And by the way," he said, pausing at the doorway. "Whatever you're cooking smells heavenly. You keep this cooking up and you're going to spoil me."

His compliment gave her a ridiculous amount of pleasure. She loved to cook. Always had, and she especially loved people enjoying what she cooked. "I hope you like it," she said simply, trying to hide her delight at his words.

Berating herself for even thinking about letting this get personal, she watched him stride out of the room. Then turned back to check on the meal: salad, smothered steak and mashed potatoes…comfort food. Most all children loved the simple food…as did most grown men.

She wasn't trying to impress Trace Crawford! She wasn't.

Twenty minutes later she stood at the door and watched him walk into Zoey's room. He was dressed in a pair of soft jeans and a plain white T-shirt. And his feet were bare as he padded across the floor. The man looked good in a pair of boots, but the casual way he was dressed right now made Paisley feel like she were looking in on a scene that was more intimate than she should be involved in. This was a family moment. And she wasn't family—and certainly didn't want to be family! Still, she couldn't tear her eyes away.

"Zoey," he called softly when she didn't look up from rocking both her bunny and two dolls. Her little arms were bulging with babies.

"Uncle," she gasped, jumping up and coming out of the tent with her arms held out.

A lump torpedoed into Paisley's throat and hot tears pressed at her eyes at the joy in the Zoey's expression. The bond Zoey felt with Trace couldn't be missed. It had started yesterday right off the bat with her shy stares and had grown through the shaky afternoon. Trace had told Paisley this morning that Zoey had had a bad dream and he'd held her for a little while until she'd gone back to sleep—even changed a diaper all by himself! Obviously the holding part had been just what Zoey had needed to understand that in Trace's arms she would find comfort.

As Paisley watched, he swung Zoey up and gave her a big bear hug. Paisley found herself remembering when he'd hugged her with such gusto. Her skin tingled thinking of it and warning bells clanged all around. She couldn't let this get personal. He may not have meant to hurt Rene, but that didn't change the fact that he had—which put anything between them off limits.

"So what's my girl been doing today?" he asked, and Zoey leaned away from him and met his eyes with her matching pair.

"Passy don't show me 'ose," she said solemnly, wagging her head from side to side, sending her curls swinging.

Trace looked at Paisley in mock horror. "She wouldn't show you the horse?"

"Uncle's 'ose," Zoey added, with a matter-of-fact nod. "You show."

Paisley crossed her arms and leaned against the door-frame as understanding passed over Trace's face. Personal feelings aside, it was a delightful experience on her part, watching the exchange. This was exactly why she'd saved the colt for Trace to show Zoey. She hadn't wanted to steal the moment away from him—when Zoey saw the colt up close for the first time. When Paisley was reading her a book about baby farm animals and their mommies, she told Zoey that her uncle also had a mommy horse and baby and that he would show them to her when he got home from work.

The toddler hadn't forgotten.

As soon as supper was over, Trace tugged on a pair of socks and boots and they all headed out to the corral. Paisley knew she should go on home now—after all, her day was done. But she really wanted to see Zoey and the colt…and Trace, so she tagged along.

With Zoey on his hip, Trace seemed genuinely more at ease than Paisley had ever expected him to be after his reaction the day before. It was amazing what a few hours could do.

When they got to the fence, he opened it, much to Paisley's surprise, and took Zoey straight into the pen. "Do you think that's wise?" she called before she could stop herself. Following them inside, she eyed the horses warily.

The look Trace shot over his shoulder held matching surprise. "Sure, it's okay. Mabel doesn't mind us looking at her baby. Now Peppy might have to get used to us but I've been working with him every day, so he's not easily spooked."

Paisley wasn't so sure as she eyed the spunky little colt prancing around the pen with his ears back and his chin held high.

"'ose!" Zoey exclaimed. Her expression registered a mixture of awe and uncertainty. The curious mom stuck her nose into Zoey's soft belly, causing her to recoil against Trace's chest in surprise.

Instantly his chuckle bubbled up and his arm tightened

around her securely. "It's okay. This is Mabel. Can Zoey say 'Mabel'?" He pushed the horse back a little so that Zoey didn't feel so crowded, but he continued to stroke the horse.

Zoey touched Mabel's soft nose and giggled. Paisley's ridiculous trepidation evaporated and she stepped farther inside the corral and pulled the gate closed. Trace knew what he was doing.

"I think Paisley needs to pet Mabel. What do you think, Zoey?"

"Passy pet 'ose," Zoey demanded, then startled everyone including Mabel when she suddenly smacked Mabel's nose with a resounding whack!

Instantly all calm vaporized as poor Mabel violently slung her head as she reared up and bolted away in a thunder of hooves.

Trace had reacted by whirling away, putting himself in between Zoey and Mabel. It was apparent that Zoey wasn't in any danger, but the scared horse had made such a commotion that the poor child erupted into wails of terror.

"It's okay," Trace said, trying to calm Zoey as Paisley led the way out of the corral. He hadn't been paying attention! He'd been too absorbed in watching Paisley enter the arena. Too absorbed in the vibrant way her hair caught the evening sun as it started to dip toward the horizon.

He should have been watching Zoey. Taking care that she didn't do something unexpected.

"Mabel didn't mean to scare you, darlin'," he crooned, cupping her head to his chest and rocking her back and forth. Paisley patted her back and put her face close so she could smile at Zoey. Trace felt Zoey's tears soaking through his T-shirt straight to his heart.

"Zoey can't hit the horse," Paisley said very gently. "The horse gets scared, too."

Zoey straightened. "'ose scart?"

Trace smiled when she turned glistening eyes to him. "Yes," he said. "The horse was just scared."

Zoey leaned away from him and looked through the fence railings. "I fowwy 'ose. No scart now."

"It's very sweet of you to say you're sorry," Paisley said, drying Zoey's tears then looking up at Trace with stern eyes.

He prepared himself for a reprimand since she had questioned his choice to enter the corral in the first place.

"Don't beat yourself up over this," she said.

"I shouldn't—"

"Button it, buster. You kept her safe. The horse didn't do anything that would have harmed her except squeal and run away."

"But I—" he started, but, eyes flashing, she cut him off again.

"Trace. You found out that Zoey has a solid slap to watch out for in the future. And I hate to be the bearer of bad news, but I can guarantee that's not the last new thing you'll learn over the next few days. Or the coming years."

Trace felt like he had a porcupine balled up in the pit of his stomach. Paisley meant the words to help him, but she had no idea that her statement didn't make him feel the least bit reassured. The future was exactly what he was afraid of.

The only reassurance that he did have was the fact that she was standing beside him. Looking into her honest eyes bolstered his sliding spirit. He gave her a nod and then forced a smile for her benefit...it was weird, though, how the smile actually felt real the instant Paisley smiled back at him.

Chapter Eight

"She hasn't mentioned Steph to me yet," Trace said on Saturday, keeping his voice low. "Has she said anything during the day to make you think she remembers her mom at all?"

They had finished supper and were walking down the drive, on a big adventure with Zoey as she made her way along, pausing to smell every buttercup and brown-eyed Susan she came across. Watching her, Paisley continued to have that overwhelming sense of thankfulness that she was so carefree and was easily settling into her new life.

"She hasn't acted like she remembers Stephanie at all. But—" she paused, placing her hand on Trace's arm "—I'm not so sure that's not a good thing for now. Look at her. She has come so far in less than a week. I was so afraid many days would be like the first day. And honestly if she did remember her mother and miss her terribly, can't you imagine how much more traumatized she would be. She would be upset and sad and she would act out those emotions in the only way a little person knows how."

"Yeah, you're right." Trace looked conflicted as he watched her. His devotion to his niece was openly apparent on his face. "I understand what you're saying, yet as mixed up as Stephanie was I still want Zoey to remember her. I mean, I can barely remember my mom." He raked his hand across his brow and bumped his hat up from his forehead with a knuckle. His eyes were deeply troubled. "I bought that book she loves so much about the baby farm animals and their mothers, hoping it would help her remember."

Paisley tore her gaze away from his profile and stared out across the pasture, blinking back her own emotions. She'd never thought about that part of it. Him not quite three with hardly any memory of his mother. Her heart wilted a little more.

"I was hoping the book would somehow help her connect to her mom. Is that crazy or what? She was one year old when she last felt her mom's arms around her…who am I kidding?" he asked. "I don't even know if Stephanie showed her any affection even then."

"I'm so sorry," Paisley said. Trace's tortured gaze reached inside of her. She wanted to smooth his brow, to show him the tenderness he'd missed growing up. She wanted to hug him for wanting Zoey to have more than he'd had. "I love what you're trying to do for Zoey." She touched his jaw, unable to resist. "I believe God truly works in mysterious ways, and I believe this is one of those times. As hard as it is to acknowledge, it's easier if she doesn't remember Stephanie. She's getting to know *you* and loving it. Her mother's memory would do nothing but distort that right now." She was saying the hard stuff. But it was the truth and she pushed on. "You're right, she was very young when social services took her away from Stephanie and you can't help that. Or change that, no matter how much you wish you could."

"You're right," he said after a moment. "But it's hard to swallow."

That a woman got herself so messed up on drugs that she neglected her child *was* hard to swallow. "Zoey is lucky to have you," Paisley said and meant it. In the short days that she'd been here, everything she'd believed about him had taken an about-face. And it was getting harder with each passing moment to keep up her defenses, to not let her feelings turn personal.

Zoey walked over and gave Trace a tiny white flower. She was beaming as she told him how pretty it was, then headed out for more leaving Trace with the tiny flower and a smile. It was so touching, and Paisley thought of the children she wanted to have one day. She found herself drawn to Trace, mesmerized by the love she saw in his eyes as he watched Zoey.

Paisley's heart went still, aching.

Later, when she left to go home, she found it hard to leave.

Sam's Diner was crowded the following Thursday night for all-you-could-eat catfish. Paisley smoothed her hand across her stomach and the slight wrinkle in the cotton material. Truth was, her stomach was kinking up in knots, and no amount of smoothing was going to get rid of them.

Trace had gotten home from work at a decent hour and asked her if she'd go to dinner at Sam's with him and Zoey. She'd said no at first because it was just so…well it was just so dangerous to her weakening resolve to be around the man all the time. But then he'd said he wasn't comfortable taking Zoey into a social evening by himself. Sucker that she was, she hadn't been able to say no to that request. After all, she was hired to help acclimate Zoey to her surroundings, *right?*

Right.

And she had been doing exactly that over the course of the first two weeks. There had been plenty of ups and downs, with not every day being a smell-the-buttercups day. But all in all Zoey seemed to be a normal little girl. A few times she'd asked about the couple who had been her foster parents for the two months prior to her coming to Trace, but then she seemed to forget them. Trace had told Paisley she'd lived with three different families in the year that she'd been in foster care, and Paisley found herself continually thanking God for getting Zoey to Trace when He did.

With every passing day it grew harder and harder to get into her car and drive away from Zoey and Trace. It was obvious that she'd misjudged him, but still, that didn't help her when it came to falling for him. She couldn't fall for the man no matter how wonderful he was. Even debating the idea made her feel she was betraying Rene.

She and Rene had dreamed of marrying and buying little houses beside each other and raising their children together. Their dream included each wearing the veil with the little Forget-me-not flowers that had been passed down through generations. Family mattered. Dreams mattered. And now that Rene lived all the way up north in Dry Creek, Montana, that dream was only an option if Paisley moved there at the end of the year. Rene had mentioned she'd heard there might be an opening at the school. Rene missed her as much as Paisley missed Rene, there was no way that Paisley would ever, ever do anything that would strain their relationship. Falling in love with the man who'd broken Rene's heart—no matter why or how the outcome had ended up—would be awkward any way you looked at it.

"Are you all right?" Trace asked, close to her ear. He'd been getting Zoey out of her car seat and Paisley had been too lost in thought to realize he'd come up behind her.

His breath sent a shiver of longing skittering over her skin and it mixed with the chill that had already come over her as she'd pondered her circumstances.

"I'm fine," she said, with determination.

His gaze drilled into her, and she knew he could see troubled waters in her eyes as she looked over her shoulder at him. He smiled though, and placed his free hand at the small of her back, leaning close as they walked into the crowded diner. "Are you sure?" he asked. "You seem nervous or something."

Oh, she was nervous! His lips inches from hers and the gentle hand touching her spine… "Just lost in thought," she said, truthfully. "Hoping Zoey doesn't get scared," she added, and focused on Zoey.

"Look who's here," Esther Mae squealed and jumped up from the table where she and her husband, Hank, sat with Norma Sue and her husband, Roy Don. "It's about time you brought that sweet baby out to meet us," she admonished Trace.

"Don't scare her," Norma Sue barked, pushing out of the booth to follow Esther Mae.

Trace tensed out of his concern as to how Zoey would react to all the attention. Everyone had been patiently waiting to meet her, understanding that she needed time to adjust.

Paisley wasn't sure what prompted Trace to decide tonight was the night for Zoey to meet everyone, but she'd known it needed to be done. All the way into town they had talked to Zoey about how she was going to meet a lot of new friends. She'd seemed fine with the concept, holding her rabbit up and declaring, "Friend."

Now, held in Trace's arms, she leaned into him and studied Esther Mae and Norma Sue. After a moment she clamped her tiny palms onto Trace's cheeks and stared excitedly into his eyes. "Friends. I not be 'fraid," she said, as if explaining the situation to him. As if trying to calm him.

"Ohhhh," Esther Mae crooned.

"If that ain't the cutest little thing," Norma Sue said.

Esther Mae nodded agreement. "Why, Trace," she added. "She's the spitting image of you!"

Zoey dropped her hands and turned back to her admirers with a wide smile. "Thanks," Trace said, beaming. "But she's much prettier than I am."

That got him a round of chuckles. Paisley watched, feeling conflicted suddenly. Just look at the man. He'd thought he needed her, but it was obvious that he and Zoey had everything under control.

And that's a good thing…right?

Right, she told herself. Sure, she reminded herself… then why did she feel such an irrational sense of sadness at the idea?

She tried to ignore the turbulent emotions churning inside her as they made the rounds. Thursday nights, the diner was filled with hometown folks. Unlike Friday and Saturday nights, which you would find a mixed group of hometown people and folks visiting for the old-fashioned theater show that was given in a renovated barn out on the edge of town. Or maybe one of the weekend festivals that they held on a regular basis. One of those was coming up in two weeks, actually, and Paisley was thinking Zoey would enjoy it. The fact that she was doing so well tonight pleased her. She just felt…what? Unneeded?

No doubt about it, she had troubles.

"Y'all look like a right smart couple," Sam said toward the end of the evening when he came by to see if they wanted any pie.

Cassie who usually helped on Thursday nights, grinned as she passed by. "You really do," she said.

"Yup," Sam continued, as he patted Zoey's head then crossed his arms over his chest and studied them. "My Adela, she can shor pickum. How you two gettin' along?"

Paisley hadn't expected this much unabashed frankness tonight. Tonight was supposed to be about Zoey…not this crazy matchmaking idea.

Trace surprised her by acting as if the statement didn't mean what she knew he understood it meant. No, he just smiled slow and easy and held her gaze—there was something in that look that reached out and touched her…and her pulse reacted and there was nothing slow and easy about the way it began racing!

"We started out on a rocky slope," he said, and she tried to concentrate on his words instead of the Olympic race happening inside of her. "But everything is leveling out nice and easy. Paisley is amazing. Isn't that right, Zoey?"

Zoey was sitting in a highchair playing with a green bean, but at Trace's question she pointed the bean at Paisley and declared in a loud voice, "Passy, *'may*-zing."

"You said it, kiddo," Trace agreed, leaning back in his chair and giving her a big twinkle-eyed once-over topped off with a teasing grin. "She's pretty 'mazing, all right."

Paisley's skin turned hot as *all* eyes in the diner zeroed in on her! How could he? Fighting for calm, she tried to find the right non-incriminating comeback. "I, I think *Zoey* is amazing, too," she managed, dropping her head and sending Trace a scathing glare from beneath shuttered lashes. Tomorrow tongues would be wagging. Didn't the man know that everyone would take that simple statement and blow their relationship all out of proportion?

Trace glanced at Paisley as he drove toward home. She'd been quiet all evening.

"Did I do something to upset you?" he asked, again. And just like she had the last time he'd asked the question she ignored him. Women—he didn't understand them.

He'd thought them going out to dinner would be a good thing. Kind of get them more on a path toward—well, a path toward…more. He wanted more and he'd thought he'd seen signs that she might have changed her mind about him. That more was a possibility.

He'd *thought* they'd been getting along good up until now. He'd gotten to where he hated to see her leave every evening, and it didn't have anything to do with Zoey. He wanted to get to know Paisley on a personal level. And after contemplating his move all week long he'd thought tonight would be a good excuse to see if she felt the same.

Obviously he'd thought wrong.

As soon as he pulled to a halt, she got out and headed toward her car. He glanced into the back seat of the truck, noted that Zoey was still sound asleep in her car seat and then he went after Paisley.

"Wait, Paisley. C'mon, tell me what I did wrong." He skidded to a halt beside her car.

"Trace, it's just time for me to go home. It's been a long day. A long week. I need to go home." She tugged her car door open. "You do remember that I have a home, right?"

He took a step back. "Sure," he said. "I know you have a home. I only meant—"

"I know what you *meant*, Trace. But you don't have to worry, you'll do fine getting Zoey out of the car seat and into bed. You don't need me to do that for you anymore. I'll see you in the morning."

She didn't waste time leaving, tossing gravel as she wheeled the old clunker she drove out of the driveway. He snatched off his hat and slapped it against his knee. "That wasn't what I meant at all," he said out loud, mystified as he watched her taillights disappear into the night.

Chapter Nine

"I need to check fence lines in the back section of the land. I want you and Zoey to ride along with me. It's a real pretty ride and it'd give me a little more time with Zoey," Trace said the next day.

Paisley had arrived at work that morning fully expecting to answer for her behavior of the night before. But Trace had been in a rush to leave and had barely stopped long enough to tell her that Zoey had a good night's sleep.

She'd had mixed feelings about his unexpected departure. It had been a relief of sorts not to have to face questions. But she'd expected questions when he came home that evening. Instead here he was telling her they were taking Zoey on a field trip.

"It sounds like a great idea," she said, trying unsuccessfully to keep the edge out of her voice.

"Great!" he exclaimed, swooping Zoey into his strong arms and heading toward the truck.

His behavior baffled her. She wanted to tell him that she was angry at him for causing almost everyone at the diner to speculate that something was happening between them.

She knew she'd entered dangerous territory where he was concerned, and no matter how many times she told herself there could never be anything between them, she was having a hard time keeping her heart from falling for the man. She certainly didn't need outside speculation, and this little excursion wasn't going to help her situation either.

She climbed into the truck while he buckled Zoey into the car seat. He was telling her all about the adventure they were about to have. Listening to him, Paisley almost smiled—it was maddening the way he got to her. She reached for her seatbelt and resolved not to weaken.

"I'd have opened the door if you'd waited a minute," he said, hopping in beside her and cranking the engine.

"I can open my own door."

"I never said you couldn't. You are formidable." He gave her a teasing grin.

"Oh, that's just what every woman likes to hear."

"Hey, I meant it as a compliment. You are capable of doing everything," he said. "But what I meant was that, for as young as you are you know a lot about kids. How did that happen?"

She glanced at him sidelong. "You do ask the strangest questions." The man baffled her completely.

He shrugged. "I'm a strange guy, I guess. But really, how do you know so much?"

"I babysat a lot growing up." She almost added that most people knew as much about kids as she did, but that would only have made him feel worse about how little he thought he knew.

"I bet you were a natural from the beginning," he said, turning the truck onto a dirt road. Glancing at her he pushed the button, letting the windows roll down. Zoey squealed with delight as the fresh air rushed inside, blowing her curls across her little forehead.

Paisley reached back and jiggled the tyke's foot, making her giggle. "I've always enjoyed children."

"So that's why you chose to become a teacher?"

Okay, so it was get-to-know-Paisley day. Not good. "Yes. Plus it was a career that would give me flexibility around my future children's schedules. A family of my own is all-important to me. And to Rene also." She might as well lay it all on the table if that was what he wanted. "Rene and I had it planned out that we would have houses beside each other one day and we would raise our kids close, like we were. We even have a beautiful veil to share, passed down from our grandmother." Paisley's throat tightened. "We've just always been close like that."

Out of the corner of her eye she saw his forehead crease below his hat and his lips flattened into a hard line. She wondered what he was thinking.

"And I came along and messed that up for you." He pulled the truck to a stop beside a low-slung barn.

Regret clearly filled his voice and she found no joy in having brought the subject up again. "But, Rene is extremely happy now," she offered and thought about sharing that they'd discussed her moving to Dry Creek—but that was too personal. She didn't want to talk about that right now, and not with him.

"So what's next?" she asked instead, glancing at the barn.

He climbed out and went after Zoey. "Now we have some fun."

Fun wasn't what she needed to have with Trace, she thought, as she followed him into the barn a few moments later. A tractor and a four-wheeler sat in the center of the metal building. Trace walked over to the utility vehicle and threw a leg over like he was climbing into the saddle of his horse. "Hop on," he said, settling Zoey in front of him.

"We're all going on that?"

He grinned over his shoulder and his eyes twinkled mischievously. "Yup."

This was not good. "But, is it safe?"

"Oh, see how much I need you. I almost forgot. Hold onto the kiddo for me," he said as he slid off the seat.

Baffled, she watched him jog to the back of the truck and pulled out two helmets, one of them a small pink one. He'd thought of everything! The helmets also meant this had been a very premeditated excursion. One didn't just pick up a pink safety helmet in Mule Hollow.

"Don't look so shocked. I didn't want to take any chances," he said as he jogged back to them. "One for Zoey and one for you if you want it."

She was dumbfounded. "And you think you're not good father material."

He looked pleased. "I have a good teacher."

Suddenly a feeling of wild anticipation came over her. She took the tiny helmet from him and smiled as Zoey blinked up at her while she set it on her head. "You have to wear this. We want to take good care of you, young lady," she explained, quickly tightening the strap.

"But you'll have fun, I promise," Trace said. "Do you want to have fun?" he asked from over Paisley's shoulder, her stomach dipping at his nearness. Zoey nodded, grabbed the handle bars and started making motor noises.

"Sounds like the kid is ready," Trace said, and giving her

a grin he swung a leg over the seat and settled in for the ride. "Hop on and let's get this party started."

"Party started!" Zoey mimicked. Trace gave her his goosepimple smile and his gaze challenged her.

She eyed the small space behind him and noted that she would have to not only sit close to him but hold on to him. A mixture of exhilaration and exclamation came over her. What was she to do? Taking a deep breath she did the only thing she wanted to do—she climbed on behind Trace and wrapped her arms around his lean waist.

Just for now, she wouldn't think about all the reasons why she shouldn't.

Within seconds they were moving across the pasture at an easy speed. Zoey was laughing into the breeze and Paisley felt like laughing herself.

"How are you doing back there?" Trace asked, glancing over his shoulder.

"Great," she said. "This is fun!"

He winked. "I like it myself," he said, watching the path in front of them again before adding. "You just keep those arms wrapped around me nice and tight and don't let go."

Paisley did as she was told, giving into the moment without protest.

"Bunny!" Zoey squealed, and just as quickly Trace cut the wheels to the right and took chase after the gray rabbit bounding across the field. Zoey laughed and Paisley held on a little tighter as Trace zigged and zagged the vehicle over the rough terrain. She found it disturbingly easy to forget everything but the moment.

"You must do this often," she said. He was driving them down an incline and her chin kept bumping him in the shoulder.

"I do but I usually don't detour like we're doing now."

The rabbit had disappeared into some underbrush, but he kept on going along a dry creek bed. When he came to a fork he brought the ride to a stop.

"I bet I know a little girl who would enjoy putting her feet into the trickle of water over there," he said.

Zoey agreed, so Paisley dismounted and watched Trace do the same. She could almost let herself imagine this was them having a good time as a family. Her arms itched to wrap around him again, her heart wished for the right to do so—what am I thinking? Getting her heart to cooperate seemed impossible as she followed Trace and Zoey toward the stream.

"Off with the shoes," Trace said, setting Zoey on a flat white rock. Zoey squealed, plopped down on her belly and reached to touch the water. Trace's laugh wrapped around Paisley, seeping into her soul as if it belonged.

No!

Her fingers were shaking as she slipped out of her loafers. She closed her eyes and prayed for the Lord to help her. To please keep her from wanting something she couldn't have.

Trace didn't make the task easy as he removed his boots and socks, rolled up his jeans and then, taking Zoey's hand, led her squealing and splashing into the ankle-deep water.

Instead of following them, Paisley sank onto the rock and dangled her feet in the water.

"Come walk with us," Trace called, holding his hand out.

He looked so appealing that her toes curled beneath the stream's surface. She shook her head. "I'll watch. This time is for you and Zoey," she said. But it was more of a reminder to *herself* that this was all about Trace and Zoey.

This was not about her. She loved Rene too much—how many times was she going to have to repeat that to herself.

Trace, with his rolled-up jeans and Zoey barely reaching his knees, made a beautiful picture standing in the stream. Paisley's heart felt as if it would die from oxygen deprivation as she held her breath and refused to let it have its way. Trace's bright, expectant expression shadowed and she knew he could see she was struggling. She just couldn't let him know what she was struggling with.

"Play wif me," Zoey said, tugging at his hand, looking up at him.

Bless her. "Play with her," Paisley repeated. Trace's jaw muscle tightened as his bottomless eyes dug deep into hers.

"Okay," he said. "But later, you and I are taking some time to talk."

So *now* the man wanted to talk!

"Fish!" Zoey exclaimed…and Paisley was momentarily saved as Trace was jerked into a hot pursuit of a passing perch.

The fish got away but it at least put Trace's focus back on Zoey. He seemed content to let Paisley remain on her rock, watching as hand in hand they waded up and down the stream in search of treasures. Paisley watched, feeling depressed.

Each time Zoey spotted a uniquely shaped rock, she squealed and brought it proudly to Paisley. One rock was shaped almost like a heart, and Paisley couldn't help slipping the small stone into her pocket as a keepsake of the wonderful afternoon.

On the way back to the barn, Trace drove with one hand and held a sleepy Zoey tucked against him. Paisley held on to him. She didn't have to, they were going so slow, but she did anyway. They traveled in silence. Paisley's head was too crowded with battling emotions to speak, and Trace seemed preoccupied also.

When he finally drove back into the barn, she hopped off the back of the four-wheeler knowing she needed distance. Distance would help her think straight.

It had been one month since he'd shown up at her house asking her to help him. One month!

No way could she feel anything for him other than infatuation—and respect, for the way he was handling his life. No way.

That was what her rational mind kept repeating. But she'd stopped thinking rationally when it came to Trace and she knew it.

She loved him.

As clear as the big, beautiful Texas sky they'd ridden beneath all afternoon, she knew it.

And she wanted to cry. Paisley had always thought that when she fell in love it would be a wonderful, peacefully exquisite feeling. That all in the world would seem right.

As she hurried to the truck, climbing inside she felt no peace. Her foot thumped against the floorboard as she watched Trace follow her out of the barn with a sleeping Zoey draped over his chest. Her little face was snuggled up against his neck, one tiny arm draped over his shoulder.

Paisley put her hand to her knee, silencing the thumping of her foot, but she couldn't silence the pounding of her heart. Nor could she help herself.

She'd fallen in love with the man who'd broken her cousin's heart.

Chapter Ten

Paisley slipped out of the house while Trace was laying Zoey down in her bed. She hadn't wanted another confrontation like the one they'd had the night before, but she also knew she couldn't talk to him.

She was heartsick. She'd cried all the way home. How had she let this happen?

She paced her kitchen floor, which reminded her of Trace, and she'd found herself wondering if he were home pacing too.

When she finally went to bed she didn't think she would sleep, but somehow she had in the early morning hours. When her alarm awakened her less than two hours later she dragged herself out of bed with determined force.

She had a job to do. And she would do it.

Today she would get her relationship with Trace back on track.

"Mornin'," Trace said, when she walked into the kitchen.

Paisley swallowed hard and tried to calm her nerves.

Trace was leaning against the counter with his arms crossed. His gray eyes, so dark they seemed almost black, were full of questions as he watched her set her purse on table.

The air crackled with strain.

"Did Zoey have a good night?" she asked.

"Slept like a rock. Look, Paisley—" he started but stopped, frustration played across his features. "What are we doing?"

Paisley's nerve wavered. "Getting you permanent custody of Zoey," she said, struggling to put them back on track.

"And the other?"

"There is no other, Trace," she said, keeping her voice level, impersonal. Feeling a stab of guilt at the surprise her words brought into his eyes.

"I see." He pushed away from the counter and headed toward the door. She could tell he was angry. "I have a long day ahead of me," he said, taking his hat from its peg and meeting her gaze.

She could see the rise and fall of his chest. It matched the tempo of her heartbeat. "I'll hold supper for you," she managed to say and tried to hold her course.

An awkward silence hung between them…but the questions were there, unspoken.

He spun on his heel and settled his hat on his head, but instead of walking out the door he just stood there. Paisley saw the tension of his shoulders bunch beneath his shirt, saw the strain in his rigid stance. She willed him to leave, knowing that him walking out that door was the safest thing. But his hand stilled on the screen.

Paisley's breath caught in her throat as suddenly he swung around and stormed toward her.

One moment she wanted to run and the next she was in his arms. Shamefully, she closed her eyes as he lowered his lips to hers. His hands came up and intertwined in her hair, and she wrapped her arms around his neck as if she couldn't get close enough to him. His muscles bunched beneath her fingertips and the feel of his lips sent her world spinning out of control. Tenderness and emotion mixed and there seemed to be no air left in the room. Paisley's heart felt as if it would fly…and break at the same time.

This could not happen and she knew it. Pushing slightly against his shoulders she pulled away from him.

Looking as dazed as she felt, he released her. His hat had fallen to the floor and he reached to pick it up. Paisley saw his hand tremble as he grasped it.

"I hope I didn't just make the mistake of my life," he said, before she could speak. "We have to talk when I get home. And I mean it, Paisley." He touched her cheek and walked out the door.

She jumped when the screen door slapped closed. Shaken, she stood in the center of the kitchen until the sound of his truck disappeared in the distance. A plan. The thought came to her as her heart settled down. She'd walked in the door with a plan and this…this made it more important than ever to get herself back on track.

Grabbing up the cup of coffee, she took a long drink of the hot liquid and hoped it burned some sense back into her.

Trace Crawford had kissed her.

And she'd kissed him back.

But that didn't change anything. Didn't change her plan.

A plan she put into action an hour later as she drove her car into town. Pete, the owner of the feedstore, was standing out front of his daffodil-yellow store in deep conversation with Applegate and Stanley. The two resident checker players must have run out of sunflower seeds and come for a refill—which was perfect for Paisley.

"Hey, guys," she called as she hopped from the car and reached in the back seat for Zoey. "Pete, I've come to buy you out of all your plants!"

"What ya need all his plants fer?" Applegate asked, his wrinkled face scrunching in question.

"Zoey, tell Mr. Thornton why we want a flower garden."

Zoey bobbed her curly head as her eyes widened. "Flowu'rs are boo'tiful."

Stanley grinned, his plump cheeks lifting. "Yup." He tweaked Zoey's toe. "But they ain't no whar' near as purdy as you, young lady."

That won him a big smile from Zoey.

Not to be beat out of a smile, Pete snapped a rose from the potted bush sitting on the sidewalk beside him and handed it to Zoey. "Here ya go, darlin'," he said, grinning when she awarded him with a dazzler of a smile. "Don't that smell good?" he asked.

"'mell *goood!*" Zoey cooed and buried her nose in the pink bloom.

Everyone chuckled and Paisley realized Zoey was going to have this entire town wrapped around her little finger before long. "I want to create a place for Zoey to explore and be able to watch butterflies and humming-birds play."

"Sounds like a good idea," Applegate said, fiddling with his hearing aid and adjusting his voice at the same time. "You ain't got much room in that car, though."

"I know y'all are probably wanting to get over to Sam's to play checkers, but do you think you could help me carry the flowers and other supplies home first?"

"Shor we can," Stanley said. "I thank a flower garden is jest what the doc ordered."

App nodded agreement, studying Paisley with disturbingly astute eyes. "It's romantic, too."

"Hey, I got a wooden bench out back," Pete said. "And I even got a birdbath back yonder. You want that, too?"

Paisley didn't need the romance part. She was having enough trouble as it was, but the bench and birdbath would be great for Zoey and Trace. "I'll take them."

"I'll back my truck up and we'll load 'er up," App said. "Heck, we kin even do some diggin' fer ya."

Paisley's heart lightened. "Thank you," she said. "Now, let's see what you've got, Pete."

Trace had spent all day thinking about coming home. He hadn't meant to kiss Paisley that morning, but after spending most of the night thinking about her and the future they could have together it had just happened.

If he hadn't just run her off.

Finding Paisley in the front yard with a shovel in her hands standing in the middle of a newly shaped flower bed that stretched across the front of his porch was not what he'd expected to find at all.

Leave it to Paisley to decide to make a change and to make it in a big way. He really loved that about her.

"What's this?" he asked, swinging a dirt-covered Zoey into his arms when she raced to meet him.

Paisley was standing to the side. Her hair was pulled back in a ponytail and she had a streak of dirt on one cheek, and her knees were dusty from kneeling.

"You've been one busy bee," he said, resisting the urge

to touch her as Zoey squirmed out of his grasp and ran to the marigolds.

"I thought you and Zoey would enjoy picking flowers and watching butterflies and hummingbirds."

"It's a great idea," he said, unable to stop himself as he lifted his hand and gently dusted her cheek with the pad of his thumb, loving the feel of her soft skin against his. "You know what I'm going to say. Thank you," he said softly, wanting to kiss her again, but knowing he'd been pushing it this morning and that he had to take this slow. The fact that she'd gone still when he'd touched her cheek made him even more cautious. Her eyes were troubled and had his heart beating with trepidation. What was she thinking? Had he messed up any chance he might have had with her?

She batted a strand of hair out of her face with the back of her garden glove. "No thanks necessary. I'm just doing my job. I've had a blast digging in the dirt all day with Zoey. You're going to have fun, too."

He took a step toward her. He could hear Applegate telling him he was being plum stupid again. But this was ridiculous.

"Whoa, cowboy," she said, "Stop right there. And don't even think about a repeat of this morning."

He looped his thumbs in his back pockets so he wouldn't reach for her. "You know I think you're wonderful, don't you?" He had to change things between them. Had to make her stop pushing him away.

"Stop."

"Paisley, I'm sorry about kissing you out of the blue. I know I shouldn't have."

She licked her lips nervously. "Look," she said, flattening her hand against her stomach. "I misjudged you, Trace. I think you are wonderful…but, this wouldn't work."

He brought his hands to her shoulders. "It can work." *If two people love each other.* His head was spinning as he watched her eyes tell him what his heart was telling him—his past foolhardy move had once again come back to haunt him. He knew before she confirmed it.

"No. It can't work. Family means everything to me, Trace. *Everything.* Don't you get it? Rene is my family."

Dear Lord, he prayed fervently. Please don't let one mistake cost me Paisley's love. "I will do whatever it takes to fix the problem if Rene has one with me. I'll get down on my knees if I have to. Paisley, I love you."

She gasped and her eyes misted. For an instant he thought he'd changed her mind then, but she looked sad and lifted her hand and touched his cheek tenderly. "I've decided that I'm moving to Dry Creek at the end of the next school year," she said, and then she moved away from him.

"What? Move?" he said. "Where is this idea coming from?"

She wrapped her arms around her waist, clearly on the defensive. "I miss Rene. She's the closest family I have left and I need to be close to her. I want my children to grow up with her children."

Trace's temper flared. He'd never thought he was going to have to compete with a childhood dream. "So that's it," he said, keeping his voice low and turning his back to where Zoey couldn't hear from where she played with her dolls at the far edge of the porch. "So all of this—Zoey, me—all we are really is just a job to you."

"Of course not. You know I care—"

"You bet I know it," he snapped, throwing away all caution. "I've seen it in the way you look at Zoey. In the small things you do that don't come in the job description.

You love Zoey. You—" He hung his head then zeroed in on her, and put it all on the table. "You look at me that same way when you let your guard down." She inhaled sharply. "You love me, Paisley. You have family here. Zoey and I are your family. I love you, Paisley Norton. You can't just throw that away all because I made a mistake."

She swung away from him and stalked across the yard. He stalked right behind her. "Rene is happy," he said. "From everything I've heard in town, Rene has married the man of her dreams, so I don't get why you think she has a problem with me. Surely she can look past my worry for Zoey and see that I made a foolish mistake, but that there was no intention on my part to hurt her the way I did."

Paisley kept her back to him and remained silent.

"Paisley. You can't hold this against me. You have been more than honest with your feelings about all of this up until now, and I've respected you for it. So I don't get this. I don't get it at all."

She spun and glared at him. "You want the truth. Then here it is. I think you want a family for Zoey so much that you *think* you are in love with me. I think you would think you were in love with any woman you'd hired for this position."

"What?"

"Don't look at me like I'm crazy. You know it's true. This has all happened too fast. First Rene, then me. You don't think you have what it takes to raise Zoey, so you want a wife. But Trace, you are a wonderful daddy to Zoey and you don't need some woman telling you what to do. You don't have to just marry someone so Zoey can have a mother. It has to be about *you* in that moment."

"That is *so* wrong," he said, still dazed that she actually believed what she was saying. "That isn't what this is about."

"You forget that I've seen terror in your eyes where that baby is concerned."

"I love you," he repeated. He raked his hand through his hair. "This is ridiculous. You can't mean this."

She crossed her arms and lifted her stubborn jaw. "I told you from the beginning that this was for Zoey. That I'd help you learn to take care of her and that's what I'm doing…but, you didn't really need me. You're a natural. And the best thing you can do for Zoey is to slow down and think about yourself for a moment." Her gaze shifted to Zoey and tears filled their green depths. "Maybe under the circumstances you should find someone else to finish out the summer."

He fought to remain calm. "You can't quit." All his life people had left him. Reality traced a frosty path across his heart. Maybe he wouldn't be able to keep Paisley from leaving, too, but he wasn't giving up that easily. "You hired on for the summer, and I expect you to be a woman of your word." He met her teary eyes with stone-cold determination.

She blinked in disbelief.

"That's right," he ground out. "I'm holding you to your word. And I'm going to prove to you that I love you."

"Why are you determined to make this harder than it needs to be?"

"I'm *determined* to do what it takes to fight for my family."

She swallowed. Blinked. Shifted from one foot to the other. She loved him. Nothing could prove to him otherwise.

And no way was he giving up on that.

"I have to go," she said, once more storming toward her car. "Tell Zoey I'll see her in the morning."

He should have felt guilty for the wobble he heard in her voice, but he didn't. He walked to the porch and picked

Zoey up. She was holding her favorite book and smiled at him as he snuggled her close. "Wave goodbye to Paisley," he said and turned her back to him so she could wave at Paisley. He wanted Paisley to see Zoey's angelic face. To see what she was attempting to walk away from.

Zoey waved and a pale-looking Paisley waved back through the window then drove down the drive away from them.

Was he wrong? Should he just give up and let her go easily out of their lives?

He closed his eyes and buried his face in Zoey's curling hair, breathing in the wonderfully sweet scent of her. *Dear Lord, let me be making the right move this time. Please show me the next move.*

Zoey squirmed in his arms, reminding him that she was his priority. With one last glance down the drive he turned and carried his baby inside. "It's time for a bath," he said, forcing his voice to sound light. Zoey chattered all the way up the stairs about her great adventures with Passy. He listened, feeling heartsick, but smiling for Zoey's benefit as he gave her a bath. Thirty minutes later when she was clean, smelling of baby shampoo and moisturizer and dressed in her soft pajamas she reached for her favorite book.

"Read," she said, yawning. It had been a long day for her and he could tell she wouldn't last long. Feeling at least a measure of contentment, he settled them into the rocking chair and opened her book. He'd given her this baby animals book in hopes of jogging a memory...but he'd given up on that. But she still loved the book; its tattered edges proved it. He placed his finger on the first page but instead of beginning to read his thoughts strayed to Paisley.

Zoey sighed against his chest and placed her tiny finger

beside his. They were pointing to the farmer's wife. "Passy, mommy."

At her words, Trace stopped rocking and his heart began thundering. "What did you say?" he asked, carefully.

"Passy, mommy," she repeated. "'ose is coat's mommy. Cat is kitty's mommy," she said, proudly, pointing at the horse and then the cat before she grinned and pointed at herself. "Passy is Zoey's mommy."

Chapter Eleven

Paisley hung up the phone and wiped her tears away. It had been over an hour since she'd left Trace and Zoey, and it felt like a lifetime. She grabbed her keys and swung open her front door and hurried down the stairs and out the apartment door. She was startled to find Trace coming up the walk.

His expression was grim. "We have to talk. Now."

"Where's Zoey," she asked, alarmed, looking toward his truck and noting that the baby seat was empty.

"I dropped her off at Norma Sue's." He wasn't wearing his hat and he raked a hand through his sandy curls and took a deep breath. "What I have to say can't be said in front of her and can't wait until tomorrow."

"What is it?"

"You're fired," he said, with all the firmness of Donald Trump. "That's what."

"Excuse me?" What?

He crossed the space between them. "As of now, you are no longer working for me."

"Oh," was all Paisley could manage, she was so shocked.

"I realized you are right when you said I was so caught up in wanting Zoey to have a mother that I lost sight of the whole picture. Also, you were right in pointing out that if I want to give Zoey what she needs then I have to know what I want. What I need. Isn't that what you told me?" he asked.

"Kind of. I guess," Paisley said, still not able to grasp the fact that he'd fired her. "You *fired* me," she said, incredulously. As in he hadn't really loved me!

"Hey, it's the only thing I can think to do under the circumstances. I think Zoey has been handed around to far too many people. First Stephanie and then all those foster parents. And then me bringing you in—it's just all too confusing for her emotionally to have so many people floating in and out of her life. Something happened after you left that made me realize I have to get this right. I can't just have you coming in and then when school starts have someone else come in. Not in her case. She's going to get hurt again if I don't fix this now."

"How are you going to fix it? And what happened after I left?"

His eyes bore into hers as he lifted his hand and laid his fingertips against her temple. Paisley's world tilted as he drew his thumb gently down the side of her face and brushed her cheek very tenderly. Looking into those dear, wonderful eyes, Paisley couldn't breathe.

"You've been crying," he said softly, and she felt his breath touch her skin.

She nodded, feeling tears threaten again. "I just got off the phone with Rene. But please tell me what happened."

"I will. Are you sure you're okay?"

She nodded, overwhelmingly happy to see him…guilt free for the first time. "I just had a good talk with her."

"Did you ask Rene how she feels about me?"

"No. I didn't ask her that."

He dropped his hands, exasperation racking his expression. "So you aren't even going to give her a chance to tell you that she's over me. That I don't matter to her future happiness and that you are free to marry me."

Paisley's heart felt as if it would explode. "Is that what you think she'd say?"

"You better believe it. The Rene I knew was upset when she left here, but she's not the kind of woman to hold a grudge. Even if she hadn't fallen in love. You know that, too. Don't you? Deep down, now that you've thought it through."

He was right. She'd been so stupid. She wanted to throw her arms around him. "That's exactly what she told me."

"Really?"

"Really, but I didn't call her to ask her how she felt about us. I'd already made up my mind about what I was going to do before I made the call."

"Really?" Trace said again, as if at a loss for words.

"Really," she said, smiling. "Aren't you curious?"

He nodded. "You're torturing me."

She laughed softly. "Then let me remedy that. I called to tell her that you and Zoey are where my heart is and that this is where I'd be staying."

Trace threw his head back and let out a whoop then swung her into his arms and kissed her as they spun in a circle. She just loved the way he did that! Laughing in relief and happiness against his lips, Paisley had been waiting for this moment for forever, it seemed.

When the world stopped spinning and he lifted his lips from hers she glared at him and gave his arm a weak slap. "But you *fired* me."

He grinned and his eyes twinkled like onyx. "Only because you seemed to have a problem with me trying to hire a mother for Zoey. I decided the only way to fix the problem was to fire you and prove to you I wanted you for my wife first. And then as a mother to Zoey."

She beamed. "What a *lovely* thing to do."

His thumbs stroked her neck. "That's me, Mr. Romantic," he whispered, sliding his palms up to cup her face. He looked at her with endearingly serious eyes. "And now that you are officially unemployed, will you, Paisley Norton, *please* marry me?"

Paisley sighed, melting against him. "*That* is my dream come true. And just so you know, I want to be Zoey's mother with all of my heart. I know you want her to remember Stephanie and I understand that—she is her mother. Her flesh and blood—"

He silenced her with another kiss and she knew he understood her heart.

"Zoey loves you, and I'll have you know she sent me after you when she told me in no uncertain terms that you were her mommy."

Paisley went still and knew she was very nearly about to become a blubbering mess. "Did she really say that?"

He gave her the goosepimple smile and his eyes twinkled. "She said it, all right. And meant it." He kissed her again, her lips, her eyes, her cheek. "How long do we have to wait before the wedding?" he said. "Please tell me you don't want a long engagement. But it's completely up to you. I'll wait," he added hurriedly, making her laugh with delight.

"Oh, Trace." How she did love this man. "Is seventy-two hours okay with you?" She watched his eyes widen in disbelief.

"Are you serious?"

She nodded, more than ready to marry this cowboy! He looked as excited as a kid and then stopped in the act of swinging her up off the floor again—the man loved to pick her up, and she wasn't complaining.

"What about your special wedding veil?"

She wrapped her arms around his neck and pulled him close, feeling their hearts beating as one, just the way they should. "This afternoon you told me you loved me. And on the way home everything became clear to me and I knew I had to call Rene. She's overnighting the veil first thing in the morning."

Trace leaned his head back and laughed and the husky sound sent her pulse racing. "I love you so much," he said, then he scooped her into his arms and strode toward his truck.

"Whoa, buster. Where exactly are you taking me?" she asked, knowing she'd go anywhere with him as she locked her arms securely around his neck. She was never going to let go of her dream come true. God was so good she could hardly believe it.

"Home. There's a cute-as-a-button little girl who has something very important to tell you."

Mommy. "In that case, can you walk a little faster?"

"Nope," he said, slowing his pace and tightening his hold on her. "This moment is mine."

"Oh, Trace," Paisley sighed and leaned her forehead against his. "In that case, take your time."

He stopped walking and looked at her with eyes so serious her breath caught in her chest. "I plan to. You are my dream come true, Paisley."

Paisley sent up a silent thank-you as she cupped her cowboy's face in her hands and kissed him with all her heart. This moment *was* theirs, and she had no intention of wasting it…or any of their moments to come.

* * * * *

Dear Reader,

We (Debra and Janet) had such fun putting together these novellas. We've noticed that a lot of the people who like to visit Dry Creek also like to drive over to Mule Hollow, and vice versa. So we consider these novellas a special summer gift to our fans. We hope you enjoy them.

When we decided to tell the story of two cousins, we talked about what would make them tick. The first cousin, Rene, has finished grieving for her deceased mother and is ready to seek her own true love. She believes love will come like a lightning bolt and she'll just know the man who she's supposed to marry. It looks like it will happen that way until she discovers that the man who she thought she was meant to marry isn't the one.

Rene learns an important lesson. God doesn't always work in the way we expect Him to—sometimes He has something even better for us.

Paisley is very protective of her cousin Rene. The last place she expects to find herself is in a situation helping the man who broke Rene's heart. But for the sake of the little girl, Paisley puts her feelings aside and by doing so finds herself exactly where God wanted her to be.

If you get a moment, let us know how you like these novellas. You can contact Debra Clopton at P.O. Box 1125 Madisonville or via her Web site at:

www.debraclopton.com.

You can contact Janet Tronstad at her Web site:

www.JanetTronstad.com.

Or you can contact Debra and Janet by writing to the Love Inspired editors at Steeple Hill Books, 233 Broadway, Suite 1001, New York, NY, 10279.
Sincerely,

Janet Tronstad   *Debra Clopton*

QUESTIONS FOR DISCUSSION

Clay and Rene

1. The hero of the first novella, Clay Preston, hates to get involved in other people's problems. Do you ever feel this way? Why or why not? There's a fine line between not being nosy and not caring. Where do you think Christians should stand?

2. Rene Mitchell, the heroine of the first novella, is brokenhearted that her plans to marry didn't work out. Can you think of similar plans in your life that didn't go the way you wanted? What happened?

3. Rene believes in love at first sight because that's the way it happened in her family history. What things do you believe about love and marriage because that's the way your parents and grandparents experienced life? Have those beliefs hurt you or helped you in your relationships?

4. When Rene realizes life isn't going the way she wants it to, she leaves Mule Hollow in search of a new life in Dry Creek. What actions do you take when you want a new start?

5. Rene stops being so upset about what is happening in her own life when she gets involved in helping a young pregnant woman. Do you believe that helping other people can heal a broken heart?

6. As Rene gets married, she wears the wedding veil that has been in her family for generations. Rene and her cousin Paisley share the wedding veil. Do you have a similar wedding keepsake in your family?

Trace and Paisley

1. Trace really made a mess of things when he asked Rene to marry him and caused her to leave town. Have you ever made a rash decision and then wished you could take it back?

2. Paisley put her own feelings toward Trace aside in order to help Zoey. Still she was reluctant to do so. But once she began to see all of the facts and motivations for Trace's behavior she was thankful God had put her there to help. Have you ever been in a bad situation turned good?

3. Did anything in this book touch your heart? If so, what was it?

4. Trace wished he could have done more for his sister— but we can't control the decisions that another person makes, even someone we love. What are your thoughts on this? Do you have any insights you could share with the group?

5. God promises that He can take any bad situation and use it for good. In this case He did exactly that. But, do you think if Trace had stepped back and prayed for guidance the moment he found out about Zoey things would have been clearer?

6. In the end of the book Trace tells Paisley that this moment was theirs and he was going to take his time and enjoy it. Do you believe couples need to take time out and make special moments just about themselves and their love? A happy, sound couple who loves the Lord and each other can face anything the world throws their way. What do you think?

When a tornado strikes a small Kansas town, Maya Logan sees a new, tender side of her serious boss. Could a family man be lurking beneath Greg Garrison's gruff exterior?

Turn the page for a sneak preview of their story in
HEALING THE BOSS'S HEART
by Valerie Hansen,
Book 1 in the new six-book
AFTER THE STORM *miniseries*
available beginning July 2009 from Love Inspired®.

Maya Logan had been watching the skies with growing concern and already had her car keys in hand when she jerked open the door to the office to admit her boss. He held a young boy in his arms. "Get inside. Quick!"

Gregory Garrison thrust the squirming child at her. "Here. Take him. I'm going back after his dog. He refused to come in out of the storm without Charlie."

"Don't be ridiculous." She clutched his arm and pointed. "You'll never catch him. Look." Tommy's dog had taken off running the minute the hail had started.

Debris was swirling through the air in ever increasing amounts and the hail had begun to pile in lumpy drifts along the curb. It had flattened the flowers she'd so lovingly placed in the planters and buried their stubbly remnants under inches of white, icy crystals.

In the distance, the dog had its tail between its legs and was disappearing into the maelstrom. Unless the frightened animal responded to commands to return, there was no chance of anyone catching up to it.

Gregory took a deep breath and hollered, "Char-lie," but Maya could tell he was wasting his breath. The soggy mongrel didn't even slow.

"Take the boy and head for the basement," Gregory yelled at her. Ducking inside, he had to put his shoulder to the heavy door and use his full weight to close and latch it.

She shoved Tommy back at him. "No. I have to go get Layla."

"In this weather? Don't be an idiot."

"She's my daughter. She's only three. She'll be scared to death if I'm not there."

"She's in the preschool at the church, right? They'll take care of the kids."

"No. I'm going after her."

"Use your head. You can't help Layla if you get yourself killed." He grasped her wrist, holding tight.

Maya struggled, twisting her arm till it hurt. "Let me go. I'm going to my baby. She's all I've got."

"That's crazy! A tornado is coming. If the hail doesn't knock you out cold, the tornado's likely to bury you."

"I don't care."

"Yes, you do."

"No, I don't! Let go of me." To her amazement, he held fast. No one, especially a man, was going to treat her this way and get away with it. No one.

"Stop. Think," he shouted, staring at her as if she were deranged.

She continued to struggle, to refuse to give in to his will, his greater strength. "No. *You* think. I'm going to my little girl. That's all there is to it."

"How? Driving?" He indicated the street, which now looked distorted due to the vibrations of the front window.

"It's too late. Look at those cars. Your head isn't half as hard as that metal is and it's already full of dents."

"But…"

She knew in her mind that he was right, yet her heart kept insisting she must do something. Anything. *Please, God, help me. Tell me what to do!*

Her heart was still pounding, her breath shallow and rapid, yet part of her seemed to suddenly accept that her boss was right. That couldn't be. She belonged with Layla. She was her mother.

"We're going to take shelter," Gregory ordered, giving her arm a tug. "Now."

That strong command was enough to renew Maya's resolve and wipe away the calm assurances she had so briefly embraced. She didn't go easily or quietly. Screeching, "No, no, no," she dragged her feet, stumbling along as he pulled and half dragged her toward the basement access.

Staring into the storm moments ago, she had felt as if the fury of the weather was sucking her into a bottomless black hole. Her emotions were still trapped in those murky, imaginary depths, still floundering, sinking, spinning out of control. She pictured Layla, with her silky, long dark hair and beautiful brown eyes.

"If anything happens to my daughter I'll never forgive you!" she screamed at him.

"I'll take my chances."

Maya knew without a doubt that she'd meant exactly what she'd said. If her precious little girl was hurt she'd never forgive herself for not trying to reach her. To protect her. And she'd never forgive Gregory Garrison for preventing her from making the attempt. *Never.*

She had to blink to adjust to the dimness of the basement

as he shoved her in front of him and forced her down the wooden stairs.

She gasped, coughed. The place smelled musty and sour, totally in character with the advanced age of the building. How long could that bank of brick and stone stores and offices stand against a storm like this? If these walls ever started to topple, nothing would stop their total collapse. Then it wouldn't matter whether they were outside or down here. They'd be just as dead.

That realization sapped her strength and left her almost without sensation. When her boss let go of her wrist and slipped his arm around her shoulders to guide her into a corner next to an abandoned elevator shaft, she was too emotionally numb to continue to fight him. All she could do was pray and continue to repeat, "Layla, Layla," over and over again.

"We'll wait it out here," he said. "This has to be the strongest part of the building."

Maya didn't believe a word he said.

Tommy's quiet sobbing, coupled with her soul-deep concern for her little girl, brought tears to her eyes. She blinked them back, hoping she could control her emotions enough to fool the boy into believing they were all going to come through the tornado unhurt.

As for her, she wasn't sure. Not even the tiniest bit.

All she could think about was her daughter. *Dear Lord, are You watching out for Layla? Please, please, please! Take care of my precious little girl.*

* * * * *

See the rest of Maya and Greg's story when
HEALING THE BOSS'S HEART hits the shelves
in July 2009.
And be sure to look for all six of the books in the
AFTER THE STORM series, where you can follow
the residents of High Plains, Kansas, as they rebuild
their town—and find love in the process.

REQUEST YOUR FREE BOOKS!

2 FREE INSPIRATIONAL NOVELS
PLUS 2
FREE
MYSTERY GIFTS

Love Inspired®

YES! Please send me 2 FREE Love Inspired® novels and my 2 FREE mystery gifts (gifts are worth about $10). After receiving them, if I don't wish to receive any more books, I can return the shipping statement marked "cancel". If I don't cancel, I will receive 4 brand-new novels every month and be billed just $4.24 per book in the U.S. or $4.74 per book in Canada. That's a savings of over 20% off the cover price. It's quite a bargain! Shipping and handling is just 50¢ per book.* I understand that accepting the 2 free books and gifts places me under no obligation to buy anything. I can always return a shipment and cancel at any time. Even if I never buy another book, the two free books and gifts are mine to keep forever.

113 IDN EYK2 313 IDN EYLE

Name _____ (PLEASE PRINT) _____

Address _____ Apt. # _____

City _____ State/Prov. _____ Zip/Postal Code _____

Signature (if under 18, a parent or guardian must sign)

Mail to Steeple Hill Reader Service:

IN U.S.A.: P.O. Box 1867, Buffalo, NY 14240-1867
IN CANADA: P.O. Box 609, Fort Erie, Ontario L2A 5X3

Not valid to current subscribers of Love Inspired books.

Want to try two free books from another series?
Call 1-800-873-8635 or visit www.morefreebooks.com

* Terms and prices subject to change without notice. Prices do not include applicable taxes. Sales tax applicable in N.Y. Canadian residents will be charged applicable provincial taxes and GST. Offer not valid in Quebec. This offer is limited to one order per household. All orders subject to approval. Credit or debit balances in a customer's account(s) may be offset by any other outstanding balance owed by or to the customer. Please allow 4 to 6 weeks for delivery. Offer available while quantities last.

Your Privacy: Steeple Hill Books is committed to protecting your privacy. Our Privacy Policy is available online at www.SteepleHill.com or upon request from the Reader Service. From time to time we make our lists of customers available to reputable third parties who may have a product or service of interest to you. If you would prefer we not share your name and address, please check here. ☐

LIREG09

Love Inspired

TITLES AVAILABLE NEXT MONTH
Available June 30, 2009

SECOND CHANCE FAMILY by Margaret Daley
Fostered by Love

Whitney Maxwell is about to get a lesson in trust—and family—from an unexpected source: her student Jason. As she and his single dad, Dr. Shane McCoy, try to help Jason deal with his autism, she realizes her dream of a forever family is right in front of her.

HEALING THE BOSS'S HEART by Valerie Hansen
After the Storm

When a tornado strikes her small Kansas town, single mom Maya Logan sees an unexpected side of her boss. Greg Garrison's tender care for her family and an orphaned boy make her wonder if he's hiding a family man beneath his gruff exterior.

LONE STAR CINDERELLA by Debra Clopton

The town matchmakers have cowboy Seth Turner in mind for history teacher Melody Chandler, but all he seems to want to do is stop her from researching his family history. Seth's afraid of what she'll find, especially when he realizes it's a place in his heart.

BLUEGRASS BLESSINGS by Allie Pleiter
Kentucky Corners

Cameron Rollings may be a jaded city boy, but God led him to Kentucky for a reason, and baker Dinah Hopkins plans to help him count his bluegrass blessings.

HOMETOWN COURTSHIP by Diann Hunt

Brad Sharp fully expects his latest community service volunteer, Callie Easton, to slack off on their Make-a-Home project. But her golden heart and willingness to work makes Brad take a second look, one that could last forever.

RETURN TO LOVE by Betsy St. Amant

Penguin keeper Gracie Broussard needs to find a new home for her beloved birds. If only Carter Alexander, the man who broke her heart years ago, wasn't the only one who could help. Carter promises that he's changed, and he's determined to show Gracie that love is a place you can always return to.

LICNMBPA0609